THE
LAST
MOVEMENT

ALSO BY ROBERT SEETHALER

A Whole Life
The Tobacconist
The Field
The Café with No Name

THE LAST MOVEMENT

ROBERT SEETHALER

TRANSLATED BY CHARLOTTE COLLINS

CANONGATE

First published in Great Britain in 2026
by Canongate Books Ltd, 14 High Street, Edinburgh EH1 1TE

canongate.co.uk

1

Copyright © 2020 Carl Hanser Verlag GmbH & Co. KG, München
English translation copyright © Charlotte Collins, 2026

The right of Robert Seethaler to be identified as the
author of this work has been asserted by him in accordance
with the Copyright, Designs and Patents Act 1988

Canongate supports copyright, which exists to encourage creativity by
making sure that authors, artists and other creative people can be fairly
rewarded for their work. Copyright allows authors control over the use and
reproduction of their work. No part of this book may be used or reproduced
in any manner for the purpose of training artificial intelligence technologies
or systems. Canongate expressly reserves this work from text and data mining
(Article 4(3) Directive (EU) 2019/790). By buying books (as well as
borrowing them from the library) you are supporting authors and publishers
and making new and original work possible.

British Library Cataloguing-in-Publication Data
A catalogue record for this book is available on
request from the British Library

ISBN 978 1 83726 521 3

Typeset in Van Dijck by Palimpsest Book Production Ltd, Falkirk,
Stirlingshire

Printed and bound by CPI Group (UK) Ltd, Croydon CR0 4YY

The manufacturer's authorised representative in the EU for product
safety is Authorised Rep Compliance Ltd, 71 Lower Baggot Street,
Dublin D02 P593 Ireland (arccompliance.com)

Gustav Mahler, head bowed, body wrapped in a warm woollen blanket, sat in his specially cordoned-off section of the sundeck on board the *Amerika* and waited for the cabin boy. The sea lay grey and heavy in the morning light. There was nothing to be seen but the seaweed floating on the surface in slimy islands, and a weird glimmer on the horizon, which the captain had assured him meant nothing at all. He sat on a steel chest, leaning against the side of a deck container, and felt the dull, regular hammering of the ship's engines beneath him. On top of the container was a coil of rope with an iron hook sticking out. The hook was rusted at the tip, the rope frayed and black with oil. Someone had told him about the smell of the sea, but it didn't smell of anything. All there was out here was the smell of steel and engine oil, and the wind, which came from the north and never seemed to change direction. Mahler liked the wind. He had the impression it blew unpleasant thoughts from his mind.

The boy approached from the afterdeck with the tea, balancing the tray on one hand and sliding the other along the railing. Mahler watched as he arranged the fine, blue-and-white porcelain pot and cup on the chest, along with a sugar caster and a little silver plate of biscuits. The boy's movements were stiff and restrained, like an old man's, but his face was smooth and childlike.

'How long have you been going to sea?' Mahler asked.

'This is my first year, Mr Director, sir,' the boy answered.

'I'm not a director, so don't call me that,' said Mahler. 'And take the biscuits away with you.'

The boy nodded. 'If you don't need me for anything else . . .?'

Mahler shook his head, and the boy left. Tiny dark leaves swam in the teapot, when in fact he had ordered Russian white. Someone had told him white tea soothed the soul. This, of course, was nonsense, but sometimes it was helpful to believe such things.

The tea was hot, and he drank it slowly. It was the only thing he would consume today. He had not felt hunger for a long time now. Perhaps he would eat again tomorrow.

The steel hull creaked beneath him, and the top of the railing vibrated. He fancied he could hear a gull screeching. But that can't be right, he thought. Six days at sea, and no land for miles around. Or is there? He would ask the captain later, or the boy.

Once he had seen a solitary gull, small and white, rocking on the waves. He had been sitting in the harsh light of a customs authority hut in New York, and while the officials questioned him about the purpose and duration of his visit, he kept glancing out at the harbour through the dusty window. Eventually he was made to sign a great pile of papers, and when he looked again, the gull was gone.

He found himself thinking about the summer three years earlier. One afternoon, he had leapt up from the wooden floor where he had been lying quietly for two hours, observing the pain in his head as it pulsated and glowed every colour of the rainbow. He stood for a few seconds, swaying, in the middle of the room, then staggered to his desk, snatched from the drawer one of the sheets of paper with the hand-drawn staves, and hastily began to scribble. A bird had called from the spruce behind the composing hut. It must have been one of those little reddish-brown ones you almost never saw, the ones the locals called 'fetchers', as it was said they brought the souls of the dead to their final resting place. The call consisted of three single notes, and, unlike the bird itself, there was nothing cheerful or sweet about them. They sounded mean. Mocking, hoarse, disjointed – but exactly right. These were the notes he had for so long failed to find, without ever really looking for them. And now here they were. All he had to do was write them down. A fourth, then a little third, rising. Mocking and mean. Then broken off. And again. And again. It was obvious what came next: down, and up again, and on, and keep going. He should have brought more of the American ink with him, he thought. The local ink was useless. It was too thin, and started to drip from the nib of the pen before it even touched the paper. Never mind – drips, blots, scribbles, he would have to make a clean copy anyway, later, this evening, at night, but right now he had to stick with it. The birdcall was the only thing that mattered.

He wrote quickly: it felt good and easy. Dear God in heaven, he thought, don't let it stop. Not before it's finished.

Three hours later, the fountain pen fell from his hand; his neck was stiff, and there was a stabbing pain in his shoulder that stretched down to his fingertips, like a tightened violin string. I wish I could keep going a little longer, he thought. Who knows whether it will come again. You can never know. For now, though, it was over.

He looked up, and was astonished to see how bright it was. The sun was shining through the window, sending beams of light filled with floating specks of dust across the room. His eyes burned; he blinked. In front of him was a heap of paper, covered in music. He would work through it at the piano that evening, or tomorrow; perhaps it would be usable. But there was no guarantee of that, either.

He placed his hands on the arms of the chair, pushed himself up and walked over to the table, where a carafe of water was meant to be, and wasn't. Same as ever, he thought. Thoughtless, forgetful, dim-witted – the country folk, Alma, the girl, himself. I should have filled the carafe this morning, he thought. Or yesterday evening. The water would be warm and stale by now, but at least there would be some.

He threw a last glance at the mess on the desk, hesitated for a moment, then stepped out into the fresh air.

It was hot outside. The sky was a radiant, cloudless blue, but it had rained in the night and the woods and meadows were lushly green. The air was full of whirring insects. A cow bellowed. That'll be the pregnant one with the black star on its forehead, he thought. Perhaps today was the day. Children were running along the road to Toblach. Their feet were kicking up dust, and he could hear their screams and laughter from where he stood. On the key rack one of the villagers had nailed to the door frame for him, where the key usually lay, and sometimes a telegram or a message from the house, sat a grasshopper with quivering wings.

Even now, three years later, he could still see the creature: the knobbly, hairy legs, the carapace at its neck, the head with the shining, staring eyes.

He was roused from his reverie by the voice of the boatswain. Every morning he summoned his sailors to the afterdeck and issued orders. The staccato shouting continued for a while, then once more there was only the steady throbbing of the engines and the swish of waves at the bow.

Mahler leant his head back. He was thirsty, his mouth was dry, and his tongue felt like a lump of wood, but he knew the tea wouldn't quench his thirst.

It must be terrible to die of thirst, he thought. But every death is terrible. Which would you prefer?

He thought of the farmhouse, high on the hill just below the spruce forest, isolated and quiet, with a panoramic view of the valley. For a long time, though, at the start of that summer, the view had remained invisible. The clouds hung low, it rained incessantly, and he spent whole days in bed listening to the water rip shingles off the roof and wash vegetables out of the earth. He couldn't even begin to think of work; the path to the composing hut had become a torrent, and it felt colder in there than outside. The spirit burner stove was too small, moss-coloured water dripped from cracks in the roof, and the damp crept into his bones and detuned the piano. So he stayed in bed. He loved his bed. The wood creaked comfortingly whenever he moved, the eiderdowns were thicker and the mattresses softer than in the city, and sometimes, just before falling asleep, he had the pleasant sensation that his body was lost in that deep, cloudy softness. Here too, though, his sleep was neither sound nor long. Ever since he could remember, he had tossed and turned throughout the night. He dreamed a lot, and although he could barely remember his dreams the next morning, they left him with a strangely troubled feeling that stayed with him for much of the day. Often he lay awake. He would hear noises in the walls, a cracking or rustling, and would get up and wander around, trying to locate the source. He brooded and worried. He thought about the music. He could feel its presence in the darkness, as if it were a living, breathing creature, its weightless body gradually expanding until it seemed to fill the whole room.

Gustav Mahler is a small, flickering flame in the storm

of his own despair. Some Viennese hack had written that about him. The 'small flame' was, of course, a reference to his delicate physiognomy and stature, barely one metre sixty. He had laughed loudly, then had torn the paper to shreds. Secretly, though, he knew the hack was right. Not yet fifty, he was already a legend: the greatest orchestra director of his age, perhaps of any age. But he paid for this fame with the calamity of a body that was consuming itself.

He had never been healthy. It ran in the family: of his thirteen siblings, six had died in infancy, so the young Gustav could already be described as a survivor. Since his schooldays he had suffered from migraines, sleeplessness, dizzy spells, tonsillitis, painful haemorrhoids, a sensitive stomach, an agitated heart. He chewed the lining of his cheeks until they bled; he gesticulated and stamped his foot uncontrollably when conducting, occasionally also while standing, or even walking. Sometimes, when he lay in bed with his eyes closed, his overwrought limbs refused to let him relax, so he would get up again and start pacing in the dark.

'You should rest,' a doctor friend had told him, years earlier. 'Preferably all your life.'

'Thank you,' he responded, then paid the bill and left. He persuaded himself that a body capable of containing so many illnesses and infirmities must be fundamentally strong. And perhaps it was actually true. In any case, he never went back to that doctor: the friendship was over.

The cold days came to an end with the arrival of the föhn. In early July, the wind swept down from the ridges of the Dolomites, bringing light and warmth to the valley. Mahler sat barefoot in the dewy grass outside the house, drinking milk and eating hunks of plain, moist bread with blackened crusts. He didn't like the farmhouse butter; he mistrusted its dull yellow sheen in the morning sun and thought it tasted ever so slightly of slurry. Rather than spread it on his bread, he used it to grease his hiking boots. Then he walked down to the village, commissioned the blacksmith to make four double-framed fly screens for the bedroom and ordered a tub of fresh, smooth, creamy butter fragrant with herbs and hay from old Farmer Karner.

The warmth was good for his joints; he enjoyed taking exercise again. He walked through the valley to Aufkirchen and Radsberg, or south to Lake Toblach, where rainbow dragonflies whirred across the black surface, then up through the gradually thinning forest until he reached the Langkofel. He kicked the heads off dandelions at the side of the road and imitated the songs of birds in the meadows. He loved the birds, and knew many of them by name. If he didn't know the name, he gave them one: practice singer, black bonnet, wild maid.

He started to work again. The composing hut was dry now; half-finished scores for the New York Philharmonic, noted down on loose sheets of paper, lay scattered over floor, desk, stool and piano, and by the end of the summer he would have finished *The Song of the Earth* and got the Ninth into reasonable shape.

In any case, he had made a start. The grasshopper sat there, motionless now. Mahler walked down to the farmhouse and in through the open front door. The old building had walls as thick as a castle's, and inside it was pleasantly cool. He stood in the hall for a moment, listening to the stony quiet. Then he took off his shoes and went up the creaking stairs in his stockinged feet.

When he entered the room, Alma was already seated. The table was laid: soup, bread, a glass of water and two small, red summer apples, shining and flawless. She will have picked out, washed and polished the apples herself, he thought. And now she's sitting here waiting, just as she has been waiting for something or someone ever since childhood, while life just passes her by. That, at least, was what she often said when she spoke of her 'half-lived life'.

He couldn't take his wife seriously in this regard;

basically, he thought she was a bit mad, at least in terms of how she saw herself. She was twenty-nine: not a girl any more but by no means old. She was still considered the most beautiful woman in Vienna, every bit as beautiful and desirable as she had been a few years ago, when she was surrounded by all kinds of men fluttering around her like wood moths around a bedside lamp.

'You're late,' she said. 'The soup's cold.'

'Never mind,' he said, sitting down. 'I like it like this, as well.'

'You've never liked your soup cold.'

'The soup's neither hot nor cold. It's just right.'

'What's the matter with you?'

'Nothing.'

'Don't you want to talk to me?'

'Yes, of course.'

'Then talk.'

'I'm working.'

'What are you working on?'

'The Ninth.'

'And?'

'And what?'

'Are you making progress?'

'I don't know. I heard a bird.'

He tapped some crumbs off the tablecloth with his fingertips and looked out of the window to where his daughter Anna was running through the grass with the local children. She was barefoot, although they had drummed into her a thousand times to keep her shoes on. The ground was still damp beneath the trees.

She's headstrong, like her mother, he thought. But what I have is happiness. One happiness is running around outside in the grass, and another is sitting here at the table with me. I have all I could wish for. I am a happy man.

He looked at Alma. Her face. The dimple in her chin where he sometimes placed his fingertip. The twitch of her eyelids. She had a habit of closing her eyes when she put a spoon in her mouth. This is what she must have looked like as a child, he thought. As a little girl.

After the meal they remained seated for a while, on the corner bench under the wooden Jesus, whose wrists and ankles were rusty from the nails. In Alma's lap lay Peter Rosegger's *Forest Farmer's Boy*. Mahler liked this book; he had put it on her pillow one morning with a maple leaf as a bookmark. But she thought it was stupid, and Rosegger a rather narrow-minded, sentimental man who made the mistake of thinking home was merely a question of provenance. Flies buzzed about the room. It's the screens, thought Mahler. They're bad. Poorly fitted, incompetently framed, full of holes and tears. The wire mesh is probably just nailed on, instead of screwed in, or at least glued. The nails are as thin as needles; they work their way out of the wood, and the insects find a way through the narrowest of gaps.

He thought of his work. He was getting there with the Ninth, but that was all. Everything was only ever getting there. Himself above all. Working meant reworking. Often, he barely finished a piece before discarding it, erasing it, ripping it up, only to start all over again. The creative spirit they were always talking about at the Opera and in Viennese artistic circles usually turned out to be just a whisperer of mistaken concepts and misguided ideas. He preferred to rely on his hearing, and, even more, on his diligence. You had to listen to things, then sit down on your backside and work: that was the whole secret.

Once, aged three, he had sat in the synagogue, squashed between his parents, and listened to the congregation singing. It was a freezing cold day; a dim winter twilight shone through the windows, and this, with the clouds of breath and the singers' false notes, created an atmosphere of dread. As the kaddish reached its climax, he couldn't stand it any longer. He jumped up, punched the air with both fists and interrupted the singing with a loud scream. In the silence that followed, he started to sing the old

Bohemian folksong 'At' se pingl házi'. His child's voice sounded desolate and shocking in that cold, high space.

Mahler listened. He couldn't hear anything in the room any more. It was as if even the flies had succumbed to the lethargy of the hot afternoon. They had vanished. Perhaps, he thought, they've gathered in a swarm up in the composing hut, and smaller swarms keep breaking away to arrange themselves on the blank pages: a crawling, whirring, buzzing score of winged notes, constantly recreating itself.

The idea pleased him. But the reality wasn't bad, either. He had been stuck at the beginning of the third movement, and the bird had unexpectedly brought him the solution. It starts with a bit of fun, a macabre joke. A mean, silly call out of the darkness, then other voices joining in, even more spiteful and silly, then footsteps, dancing, marching feet, a stamping and staggering, a running and rushing, drunkenly, blindly flinging themselves into a maelstrom that can only lead to the abyss.

He laughed softly, and shuddered at the same time. Suddenly it was too claustrophobic in here, the upholstered chair too soft, the air too stuffy, and the flies seemed to be back now after all.

And then an idea comes to him, or the shape of an idea, perhaps no more than an inkling: a double beat theme, rising to fortissimo then dropping to pianissimo, on and on, trickling away, slower and slower, fading until it becomes inaudible. He opens his eyes and stares at his wife; the book has slipped from her lap and fallen to the floor.

'I think I've got it,' he says. 'It's a dissolution. A falling silent for all eternity.'

But Alma doesn't reply; she is asleep.

Mahler shivered. A slight breeze had arisen. Perhaps the *Amerika* was accelerating to make up time. But what time? The sea was still calm. He would have liked to see some fish. People had told him about fish with silver wings that broke the surface and sailed hundreds of metres through the air. Sometimes gulls would catch them and eat them in flight. But there were no flying fish here, and no gulls, either. There was only water and forty thousand tonnes of steel. Perhaps the flying fish were just a myth.

He raised his legs with an effort and wrapped the woollen blanket more tightly. The cool air out here was doing him good; his fever had gone. But it would come back, and with it the aches and the waking dreams. The tea had gone cold. He rang the little hand bell and was surprised, as ever, to see the boy appear just moments later.

'You can't possibly have heard it in this wind,' he said.

'But I did,' said the boy.

Mahler considered him. In his uniform jacket and cap he looked like a schoolboy in disguise.

'Have you ever seen flying fish?' he asked.

'Yes, you see them all the time.'

'I don't.'

'I'm sorry to hear that.'

'Nothing for you to be sorry about.'

'Oh, but there is – it's the most beautiful thing you get to see out here.'

'I thought that was the sunrise.'

'Sunrise, and the flying fish,' said the boy. 'Old men say they're the souls of the drowned. That they can't get used to the dark, and go looking for the light.'

'And when they find it, they get eaten by gulls.'

The boy shrugged.

'Do you believe the story about drowned souls?' Mahler asked.

'I think they're just fish,' said the boy. 'But I don't know for sure. Who knows what goes on down there.'

Mahler gazed out over the sea, which still lay grey and empty. Yes, who knows, he thought. Foolish notions.

'Can I do anything else for you, Mr Director, sir?'

'Yes. Throw me in the sea.'

'I'm not sure I understand . . .?'

'Never mind. Bring me another tea.'

'Certainly, Mr Director, sir!'

The boy left, and Mahler's thoughts turned to Alma and little Anna. They must already be having breakfast downstairs. Anna was six, and loved the dark, bitter marmalade you only found on big ships and in hotels. Children never liked this marmalade, but Anna couldn't get enough of it. She spread it in thick layers on her bread and laughed as she bit into it, grinning from ear to ear. She didn't laugh much otherwise. She had an eye for beauty, but she viewed the world with seriousness and a certain detachment. She was filled with thoughts and idiosyncratic ideas. Sometimes she would sit in the garden making tiny musical instruments out of little bits of wood and blades of grass and teaching the insects to play. In winter, there were days when she would suddenly start to cry, and if you asked her why she was so sad, she didn't answer.

She was different from her sister Maria, who would have turned nine this year. Mahler found himself thinking of the day he had first held Maria in his arms. She had seemed incredibly light. It was as if someone had handed him a bundle of cloth. This creature on his arm was completely alien to him, yet he was amazed by the love he felt for it.

The first cry had filled him with horror. But when they called him into the room and he saw the doctor's face, he felt happier and more relieved than ever before in his life. Alma was lying in bed looking out of the window, to where wild ivy straggled over the frame. The female attendant leant over her and drew a symbol on her forehead with a thumb. It had been a breech birth, the doctor said, but it was all over now and both were healthy. Mahler knew he had started laughing and said something, but he couldn't remember what.

Later, everyone had sat around the bed, unable to take their eyes off the tiny face lying amidst the white cloths like a wizened red fruit. Beside her, Alma lay with her long hair loose about her head, hands heavy and motionless on the crocheted blanket. She had never appeared more beautiful to him. And he had never felt more superfluous. He tried to spread good cheer, joking about the baby's wrinkled eyelids and the navel that protruded from her belly like a tail. The little tail had popped out in front, he said, because they'd slapped her bottom too hard. Everyone laughed, including Alma, and he laughed loudest of all. The attendant said that the baby's toes had moved like fingers as she was pulling her out. As if she were waving hello with her tiny toes.

'And now she's here,' the attendant said. 'And she won't be leaving anytime soon.'

Maria was a cheerful child. Mahler remembered her exhilaration when she jumped into the lake and splashed about in the water with her thin arms, laughing and spluttering. Once, he had swum with her on his back almost to the middle of the lake. She had stuck to him like a frog, arms wrapped around his chest, her cheek nestled against the back of his neck. He was moved by her absolute trust and her small, light body on his back, and could have wept for joy if the swimming hadn't been such an effort. Occasionally he heard her laugh softly on his back, but he didn't ask what she was looking at or what she was thinking. He just kept swimming, and it felt as if they were the only two people in the world.

When they got back to the shore, Alma met them with tears and a tongue-lashing. She said he was the most irresponsible person who had ever lived. It was bad enough that he always swam too far out in this wretched lake when he was alone; now he had to take the child with him too, and put a whole family in danger? What had he been thinking? Nothing, probably. Of course not. Just put your little daughter on your back and jump into the water. That was how he was: thoughtless and stupid. The famous Gustav Mahler, a thoughtless, stupid man who risked the life and happiness of his loved ones for a few moments of splashing around. She scolded him all the rest of the day. Only after the girls had gone to sleep, as they sat together on the balcony gazing out over the lake that lay still before them in the twilight, did she calm down.

'You are an idiot,' she said. 'And I love you. Promise me you won't do it again.'

'I promise,' he said.

That was almost exactly a year before Maria died. One day she complained of a sore throat. She was shivering, and had a temperature. Her sister Anna had developed scarlet fever a few days earlier; to prevent the illness from spreading, she had been taken to her grandparents' house, where she soon recovered. Then Maria fell ill. It was diphtheria, but the name of the illness was unimportant. She fought for ten days, and died in the early morning. Mahler ran into the forest and wept and screamed. By the time he came back and sat down with Alma and her mother, who were huddled together like frightened animals, something inside him had hardened. He sat there, wide-eyed and silent, staring out of the window.

Four years had passed since then, but the

memory of it was so clear that he thought he could hear Maria's voice, her gurgling, rattling breath in that room in the house by the lake.

He sat up and reached for the bell, but didn't ring. What would he have said to the boy? He sipped the tea, which tasted strong and sweet, and leant back again. Don't think about it, he thought. It's not right to think about death. Death is nothingness. Think about the flying fish. When would they finally show themselves? How much longer did he have to sit here on deck staring out over the water? The sea had not changed. A vast indifference. Silent and stupid. What was it to him? He was shivering, but he felt hot again; the fever had returned. He wrapped the blanket tighter around his legs and tipped back his head. His eyes ached; the wind was making them dry. He dipped a finger in the tea and ran the damp fingertip across his eyelids. He was so tired. He longed for sleep, and yet he feared it. I should have composed a song of sleep, he thought. Or a whole song cycle. The realm where demons appear. I could have composed so much more. It feels as if I've only just begun, yet it's already over. So this is what dying is like, he thought. Hold still and wait.

They never went back to the lake. Instead, from then on, they spent the summer holidays in Toblach, in South Tyrol. From the farmhouse they could see right across the valley; they had the composing hut built for him under the spruces, and the piano hauled up. He could work again. Sometimes he thought he heard Maria's voice in the forest, or saw something that looked like a corner of her dress whisk past the window.

'If that's you, come in,' he would say. 'If it isn't, don't come here again.'

Before heading to New York at the end of the second Toblach summer, they had travelled back to Vienna. He thought of how he had stood at the window of their old apartment while the furniture was being packed behind him for transportation to the depot. He had acted as if none of this concerned him any more, staring down at the street he had run along so many times, spurred on by haste, or sometimes by his fury at the orchestra, the choir, the blockheads in the administration, all the lazy, lying, two-faced rabble at the Vienna Court Opera whose director he had been for ten years.

It was in the spring of 1897 that he first stepped into the director's office overlooking the Ringstrasse without the accompaniment of some court lackey. The room was stuffy and smelled of dusty paper; the window was screwed firmly into its frame and could not be opened. The night porter had told him this was intended to prevent directors leaping up from their office chairs in distress and jumping straight out onto the opera house courtyard.

Mahler sat down at the desk, a huge black monolith that reminded him of a Viennese family grave in the Central Cemetery, and for a brief moment he was overcome by the definitive, irrefutable certainty of his impending failure. Then he set to work.

In his first season he conducted one hundred and nine performances; he was still conducting around fifty in his last. Before his arrival, the singers had stood at the front of the stage, stiff and impassive, singing down at the audience. Now they had to learn to think of themselves as part of a greater whole and integrate accordingly. The new director required them to activate their body and personality (or what they thought of as such) and start acting, no more and no less. Anyone unwilling or unable to do this was relegated to the choir or sacked. He drove out the claqueurs, dimmed the lights in the auditorium and lowered the entire orchestra pit to improve the view of the stage. For the first time, the operas were presented in such a way that you could actually follow the story. Music, poetry, space, light, movement – all were one, and the synergy between them gave a deeper meaning to the whole than the mere juxtaposition of individual elements had, until then, been able to achieve.

He thought of how quickly the disquiet in the opera house had spread across the city. Within a few weeks, word had got around that something out of the ordinary was going on, and of course everyone wanted to be in on it. The Viennese were of a fundamentally hot-tempered disposition: beneath their comfortable, well-fed exterior, enthusiasm and outrage seethed in equal measure and constantly threatened to bubble over at the slightest provocation. In the street and in the coffee houses people quarrelled over the repertoire, argued about the temperament and sound of the orchestra or mocked the female singers' physiques. Many performances sold out; on premiere nights young men would come to blows, fighting over the last remaining tickets. People wanted in on it. They wanted to be part of the conversation. Above all, though, they wanted to see the fidgety little Jew who had inexplicably contrived to discipline the best and most intractable orchestra in the world.

Mahler thought back to those days with quiet astonishment. How young he had been back then. It felt like a lifetime ago. You play a note, and it continues to vibrate in the room. Yet it already contains its own end.

Downstairs, the removal men were walking back and forth between the front entrance and the waiting trucks with pieces of furniture on their backs. One of them, a thickset, red-faced fellow, bore a rocking chair high above his head like a trophy. Another carried in front of him a gently tinkling chandelier with opulent cut-glass decoration. Mahler couldn't recall ever having seen this chandelier before. In fact, he had the impression that he was seeing many of these things for the first time. Perhaps he was. He had once heard that over the course of a person's life every cell is replaced several times over, so that after only a few years nothing of the original body is left. A sort of continual rebirth in miniature. But if the individual parts were constantly being exchanged, could you still accept that there was any sort of continuity to the whole? A consistent self whose core and essence remains immutable over time? Was the world-famous conductor Gustav Mahler still the same person as the young, freshly appointed director of the Court Opera who once sat beneath this chandelier, on that rocking chair? Or the six-year-old Jewish boy with a shallow crown hat in his hand and an infinitely sad expression in his eyes pictured in the photo that Alma had just plucked from a drawer, saving it from transportation to the furniture depot?

A velvety layer of dust had accumulated on the window over the summer. He sketched some lines and notes in it with his finger. D flat major. Not uninteresting. Adagio, of course. Petering out. Trickling away. And violas. Yes. It has to be the viola. It ends with that. With that it begins all over again.

Once the last pieces of furniture had been loaded up, the workers had been paid, and the trucks had roared around the corner and disappeared, he and Alma stood for a while in the empty space that had once been their home.

'It was good,' said Alma.

'What was?' he asked.

'Everything,' she said. 'Everything here was good.'

A few days later they left for Paris. Mahler thought about how enchanting the city was. Pure kitsch. The Champs-Élysées basked luxuriously in the autumn light, and the women of Paris paraded the latest millinery, voluminous creations as delicate as candy floss, undulating gently in the wind.

Here, too, Alma was a phenomenon: taller and more voluptuous than most Parisiennes, a woman who compelled the male gaze, and that of other women even more so. The small, slender man at her side attracted no attention. No one recognised him, and he was fine with that. He didn't want to be recognised, he didn't want to be spoken to, and, in any case, all the cheerful gushing and affectation got on his nerves.

It had already been like this in the April of that year, when they stopped off in Paris for a few days en route from New York to Toblach. It could all have been so lovely: the gruelling season had come to an end, the interlude at the Metropolitan Opera was almost over, and springtime in Paris is even better than autumn. However, a few months earlier, Alma's stepfather had had the daft idea of commissioning a bust from Auguste Rodin for Mahler's fiftieth birthday. Mahler didn't want to do it, but Alma and Claire de Choiseul, Rodin's indefatigable muse, were extremely persistent, so there was endless cabling back and forth, cancelling and confirming and cancelling again, before they finally agreed on a price of twelve thousand francs and arranged some sittings at Rodin's studio.

All this came back to him as they crossed the Pont Alexandre III again that autumn. In the spring, on their way to the initial sittings, the water had glittered so brightly that it hurt his eyes; now the Seine shimmered a dull silvery blue. They walked down the Avenue du Maréchal-Gallieni towards the dome of Les Invalides, then turned into the rue de Grenelle, and after crossing the Boulevard des Invalides they reached the rue de Varenne, where he stopped beneath a chestnut tree and refused to continue.

'We'll be late,' said Alma.

'Fine by me,' he said.

She looked at him and jutted her chin. 'Other people would pay a lot of money for this. Much more than we paid. I wish you could see it like that. It's something that will endure. Something people can look at and touch. And, anyway, I'll be with you. I'll sit with you the whole time. It'll be over soon, you'll see. Good grief, it's only a couple of hours.'

'I'm hungry,' he said.

'We had breakfast less than an hour ago,' she said. 'There was tea, croissants, Corsican honey, butter, poached eggs, salmon and black bread. You ordered two extra helpings, and I spread honey on your bread.'

'You don't understand me. You don't even try to understand me.'

'I don't know if it's actually possible to understand you. But if it is, there's no one who understands you better than I. There's not a soul in the world who knows better than I who you are and what you can be like. And that's not always easy, believe me!'

'Well, then, it's not easy. I shouldn't have come here, anyway. This city drives you mad. All cities drive you mad. You walk around and don't know what you're actually doing here. I have no idea why I agreed to this idiotic business. That Rodin is a madman.'

'He's the greatest sculptor of our age.'

'He's a peasant. Coarse, dirty and loud.'

'You're terrible.'

'Life is terrible. So why shouldn't I be? Was it

my idea? What have I got to do with it? You could have asked me whether I actually wanted a bust. I would have told you no, thank you, I don't want one. If I feel like seeing myself – which, by the way, I never do – I can look in the mirror. We should have stayed longer in Toblach. Or Vienna, as far as I'm concerned. I could be sitting in the forest now, composing. Or in a coffee house, thinking. Or we could have taken an earlier steamer. We would have been in America for a while already, and we wouldn't have to walk around this saccharine city.'

'Do you actually know how hurtful you can be?'

He looked at her face, contorted with annoyance. A loose strand of hair hung down over her forehead, and her cheeks were flushed. He couldn't help it: he loved her.

'I slept badly,' he said. 'That's all. You should all just leave me alone.'

'And then what?' she asked. 'What would happen then?'

He could hear the birds above them, and the tiredness in him was so overwhelming that he would have liked to lie down on the grass and stare up into the tree without thinking anything else.

'I'm sorry,' he said. 'Things aren't always as easy as they could be.'

'I know,' she said.

'I don't believe you.'

'Fine. Believe what you like. Now let's go.'

Mahler raised his hands, then dropped them again and marched on ahead.

Rodin's studio was in the Hôtel Biron, a former mansion built for some aristocrats in the eighteenth century that, over the years, had become so dilapidated that it was practically a ruin. Mahler hated it from the moment he walked in. Everything about the building was repulsive to him, especially the huge garden, which he felt resembled a jungle where at any moment wild animals might burst from the thickets and spring at his throat. Great birds shrieked invisibly in the treetops and colourful butterflies reeled in the sunlight. A one-legged girl in a shimmering, mother-of-pearl silk nightdress was standing on a boulder with her back to them.

'Good morning, mademoiselle,' said Alma. 'Is the maestro at home?'

The girl didn't even turn her head. Now Mahler saw that the boulder was in fact a roughly hewn block of marble: a mangled torso, contorted features, mouths open in a scream. And he saw that the girl had raised her other leg up high, propped it on the block, and was gently stretching her muscles, cheek resting on her calf. The sinews of her neck stood out like thin wires.

'Eh! Bonjour!'

Rodin was standing in the grass some way off, waving. His hand in the sunlight was huge and white. Mahler remembered shaking it when they said goodbye in April; it was dry and hard, as if it too were hewn from stone. Despite the warm weather, Rodin wore a thick tweed suit, and sweat was trickling from beneath his top hat. It was impossible to make out whether or not he was smiling. His beard was shaggy and unkempt and extended well past the third button of his shirt.

'Bonjour, monsieur! Bonjour, madame!'

'Bonjour,' said Mahler. 'How long do we need?'

They went into the studio, and Rodin started work, which consisted of kneading little balls of clay between his fingers, applying them to the model and shaping them. His hands moved like independent creatures as he did so; Rodin didn't seem to pay them any attention. He stared out of the window and appeared to be watching the clouds above the trees as his fingers shaped an ear, the forehead, the side of the nose, only to destroy it all and start again from scratch in a single movement. Sometimes he closed his eyes.

For Mahler, sitting on a stool and forbidden to move, these moments when he was not being observed were the most bearable. He used them to conserve his strength by first sagging briefly, then sitting bolt upright and tensing the muscles in his back until they shuddered. For some time now he had had pain in his back and right shoulder. When he was conducting he didn't notice it, but the moment he sat still, or when he lay down in bed at night, all the joints in his body seemed to seize up, and the pain travelled from the middle of his spine to the tips of his fingers and toes. On one occasion he had been to see a Tyrolean physiotherapist about it, who had pressed so hard between his shoulder blades, first with his knuckles, then with his elbows, that Mahler had had to bite the pillow to smother his cries of pain. The treatment didn't help, and he did not go back. Since then, he had tried to adapt to his body's unreasonable demands.

Alma sat in one corner of the room, Claire de Choiseul in another. The two women had greeted each other with a quick exchange of air kisses and a few civilities, and had not looked at each other again.

Mahler gazed out of the window and wished himself far, far away. Life was happening outside. Not in here. Here, a muffled, unpleasant silence reigned. The only sounds were the creaking of the stool, the squelching of the clay in Rodin's hands, his wheezing breath. The air was warm and stifling. It was as if the clay that lay all around, in lumps or worked up into rough sculptural models, had sucked all the moisture from it.

He cleared his throat. 'I could do with a glass of water.' His voice sounded strangely unfamiliar in these surroundings.

Rodin slapped a piece of clay onto the model and dropped his hands in his lap. 'Comment? Qu'est-ce qu'il y a?'

'Water,' said Mahler. 'I'd like a glass of water.'

Without a word, Rodin stood and left the room. Suddenly there was noise outside. Clinking and clattering. Shouting. The barking of several dogs. Footsteps stamping back and forth.

'What's going on?' asked Mahler.

'Nothing important,' said Madame de Choiseul. 'You mustn't take any of it too seriously.'

'Oh, there's no chance of that,' said Mahler.

The door opened and Rodin came back in. The glass of water was like a tiny shot glass in his hand. Mahler knocked it back in one. It tasted like everything else in Paris: rather insipid. He thought of Toblach, the fat drops that hung from the spruce needles first thing in the morning, cool and pure and fragrant. Each drop carried within it the taste of a whole forest. He thought of how he had once spent half a day on the wooded slopes beneath the Haunoldköpfl. After a long time clambering through the undergrowth, at some point in the afternoon he had stretched out on a mossy slab of rock and fallen asleep. When he woke, he saw a falcon sitting in the tree above him. The hawk had a dead pigeon in its talons and was plucking feathers and bits of skin from the body with its sharp, hooked beak. It sat completely still, jerking only its head as it tore at its prey. The pigeon's head dangled, and the feathers floated slowly down through leaves and branches to the ground. Mahler sat up, and the falcon paused for a moment to ascertain whether it was in danger, then soared up high into the air with just a few wingbeats, the pigeon in its talons also seeming to flap its wings one last time.

He had stayed in the forest for quite a while longer, and when he finally set out for home at dusk he was still thinking about the falcon and the pigeon and the dry, papery sound their wings had made in the sky above the trees.

He laughed out loud.

Rodin slapped a lump of clay onto the model and said something unintelligible.

'Excuse me?' said Mahler.

'Would sir please be so kind as to sit still?' translated Claire de Choiseul.

'Yes, all right,' he said.

'No, it's not all right,' said Claire. 'We want to make progress with the work, after all.'

'Who's *we*?'

'All of us in here, and most of the people out there,' said Claire. 'If we're not making progress in here, the world outside turns more slowly.'

'Hopefully it'll soon stop turning altogether,' said Mahler. 'That'd solve the problem.'

'Don't listen to him,' said Alma. 'He's a bit tired.'

'No, I'm not,' said Mahler. 'I've never been more awake in my life.'

'Tais-toi!' said Rodin. 'Tais-toi, putain!'

'What's he saying?' asked Mahler.

'Once again, he politely requests that you sit still,' said Claire. 'The day isn't over yet.'

'It looks as if it'll never be over,' said Mahler. 'But all right, I'll sit still. For ever.'

'Please, Gustav,' said Alma. 'Pull yourself together!'

'Why? That's the solution. Sit still for all eternity. Then you can embalm me, or stuff me, or both. It'll save all the work on the bust. Not to mention the cost of the materials.'

'Ignore him,' said Alma.

'We're trying,' said Claire.

'Not hard enough,' said Mahler.

'De quoi ils parlent, ces idiots?' asked Rodin. His eyes were bloodshot, and around his mouth his beard was twitching.

'De rien,' said Claire. 'Monsieur fantasme sur la mort.'

Rodin nodded. Then he got up, went over to a half-finished sculpture of a satyr emerging from the ground and kicked it with all his might. He only calmed down when Claire cautiously approached him from behind, put her arms around his neck and started whispering to him, quietly but with apparent urgency. Without another glance at the broken satyr, Rodin returned to the bust. He kneaded the hairline once more, stroked his index finger across the forehead, then slumped, wheezing, and closed his eyes.

'Now what's the matter?' asked Mahler.

'The maestro has finished,' said Claire, rising from her chair. 'Now it must dry, and then it will be cast. The bust will be sent to you by post.'

'There – it all worked out in the end!' cried Mahler, leaping up from the stool. 'Alma, let's go!'

The sun was higher in the sky now, but it was still cold. Mahler rubbed his hands and slipped them back under the blanket. Cold is good for the fever, he thought. It's nice out here. I can bear it as long as I want.

At his request, they had carried him up before dawn and prepared his usual spot for him. The beauty of the sunrise had brought tears to his eyes, and he had sent away the boy, who had been standing next to him, half-asleep. He himself had been surprised by this. He'd thought he had overcome any sense of shame long ago. More and more often of late he'd had to let strangers carry him, wash him, dress him and put him to bed; it had always been done discreetly, with a kind of professional matter-of-factness that left no room for feelings like shame or embarrassment.

And then he was ashamed of shedding a few tears in front of a child in an outsized uniform.

Suddenly he could feel the lazy rolling of the ship. A kind of internal swaying, light and sluggish. On big steamships you soon forgot you were at sea; it was only occasionally, particularly in a heavy swell, that it occurred to you there was nothing beneath you but cold black water.

Although he had crossed the Atlantic many times, he couldn't get used to this idea. 'The sea is never your friend,' an old sailor had told him once. 'It doesn't want anything good or bad. It doesn't want anything at all. It has no intention whatsoever when it kills you with the single blow of a wave.'

The man was the captain of the *Kaiser Wilhelm II*, which they boarded in Cherbourg after the Rodin episode. 'She's a marvel, isn't she?' he had called out in greeting, as Mahler craned his neck on the gangway to get a good look at the full scale of the ship. 'Nothing more than a lump of welded iron, but a marvel!'

On the crossing, Mahler spent most of the time alone in his imperial suite. He didn't want to be disturbed, by anyone or anything, not even little Anna, except perhaps early in the morning, when he would spend a few minutes playing with her on the mattress. Apart from that, he requested absolute peace and quiet. He had a demanding season ahead:

he had to rehearse a new production of Tchaikovsky's *The Queen of Spades* at the Metropolitan Opera, programme more than forty concerts with the Philharmonic, study the scores and find the instrumentalists. Sometimes, when the sea surged outside and the ship began to roll, he would lie down flat on the elegant, star-patterned parquet floor and listen to the pounding of the engines and the roar of the sea, until the swell, or at least his nausea, subsided and he was able to go back to work.

Now, in his mind's eye, he saw them sailing into New York harbour. The city rose up out of its mist. A monster, and at the same time so beautiful it took your breath away. Once again, New York appeared to have grown. Where in the spring a wide gap had revealed a vista of avenues, there was now a building with frameless windows and a pointed roof of gleaming silvery steel plate. The Park Row Building was one hundred and nineteen metres tall, the recently completed Singer Building one hundred and eighty-six, and behind it was the Metropolitan Life Tower, two hundred and thirteen metres high. Surely this would have to stop soon, he thought. Impossible to build even higher. Impossible for the marshy ground beneath the city to bear the weight of such giants in perpetuity.

On the gangway, Alma stumbled over the hem

of her dress and narrowly escaped falling into the water of the harbour, which New Yorkers said was so filthy that even rats fell down dead and their stomachs burst open if they so much as came into contact with it. He recalled the terror in her eyes, and her warm breath on his cheek as he caught her and pressed her to him until their feet were on solid ground.

In one of the New York Taxicab Company's yellow Thomas 4-20s they drove right across town to the Savoy, where all the staff and a great many others had gathered in the lobby to greet them. Hello! Welcome back! Great to have you here! Handshakes, pats on the back, hugs, baskets of flowers, tickets, cards, telegrams. A girl in a sequinned dress presented Alma with a bouquet of white orchids. Alma lifted the little girl up and spun her round in a circle. Everyone laughed and clapped. Then there was champagne. A delegation had come from the Philharmonic. A division of the ladies' committee. Cigar smoke and clouds of perfume. Stiff hats and rustling gowns. The Americans' enthusiasm appeared genuine: the European maestro is back!

The reception had pleased him. At the same time, it was unbearable. He didn't know where to stand or what to say. He smiled, shook hands, waved.

'Thank you!' he kept repeating. 'Thank you very much!'

Later, he and Alma stood at the big corner window of their ninth-floor apartment, looking out over Central Park with its small zinc-grey lakes and trees that seemed to glow in the evening light. Down on the plaza, everything was in turmoil. The world had grown loud, and New York was the epicentre of the noise. Everywhere there was arguing and shouting; people rushed and ran about as if fleeing from something. Instead of horse-drawn cabs, automobiles hurtled along the streets; you hardly ever saw stray dogs any more. A woman wearing a fur hat was pushing a handcart with hot lemonade, striking two little bells repeatedly as she did so: *ding dong, ding dong*. A man and a woman crossed the street. The woman threw back her head and laughed. She stumbled and took the man's arm; he stopped and looked at her for a moment, then they turned the corner and disappeared. The sun was going down behind the Park Theatre. The billboard on the façade began to flash: *Old Quaker Rye Whiskey.*

'It's beautiful,' said Mahler. 'If we can only grasp it.'

'You say that whenever you stand at a window,' said Alma. 'Or at the top of a mountain, or a church tower, or anywhere with a view.'

He shot her a sideways glance. She had leant her forehead against the glass and was gazing out over the park into the distance. He stood there for a while, uncertain, then put a hand on her hip.

'Come,' he said. But she didn't move, or reply. 'Let's go to sleep. It's late.'

'The sun's going down over there.'

'As I said, it's late.'

'You know, I like American beds. They're quite high, and you can hear the feathers squeaking. But they're softer than the ones at home.'

'I like the beds, too. Come on.'

'Sometimes I feel they might even be a bit too soft. They give you backache.'

'I'll get backache if we stand here much longer.'

'Look at the sun. It's just a sliver of red now. But there's still strength in it. We should be grateful for each day. Let's do it differently this time, shall we? We've seen so little of America. This vast country. We don't even know this city. They have "drugstores" everywhere. On every corner. This is our third season and I've still not been to a drugstore.'

'We'll go tomorrow.'

'Promise me?'

'Tomorrow, straight after rehearsal, we'll go to a drugstore and buy something. I promise. Now come to bed!'

Later, when she had fallen asleep with her head facing the window and her long, tousled hair fanned out across the pillow, he lay there and looked at her. The bluish radiance of night lay on her face. There is no one else, he thought. She is my happiness. I don't know whether I am hers, but she is mine. I don't know whether I've earned her. You can't earn love. Look at her. Her shoulder, like a mound of snow. Rodin is a dilettante. All art is dilettantish. Her forehead. And her mouth. And this bit here. I wish I could see her dreams, he thought. But it's probably better this way. It isn't good to know everything. There are no dreams, only this face. A face like this stays young, and it makes you old. I'm an old man, but there's still life in me. I can hold on a while longer. I should stay awake and not look at anything but her face. And the rest. It's enough to drive you mad. I must sleep. These idiots: an orchestra isn't all fun and games, someone has to take charge. And tomorrow she wants to go to a drugstore; no idea what that is, but don't forget. Don't forget, don't forget. Look at her, lying there, absolutely still.

The next morning, right on time, he stood before the musicians of the New York Philharmonic and conducted the first movement of the *Eroica* and Liszt's second piano concerto. They didn't have much time until the first performance, so he skipped the speech of welcome and all the other little courtesies and plunged straight into the first rehearsal.

This didn't surprise anyone; after all, he had the reputation of being something of a demon on the podium. The musicians respected and were scared stiff of him. Which was just as well, because most of them were clearly phlegmatic individuals who didn't know the first thing about art and were scarcely capable of distinguishing a violin from a viola. Here and there, this swamp of mediocrity did occasionally put forth a delicate bud of musicianship, but all in all this orchestra was a profoundly vacuous, hopeless affair.

He set about his work like a madman. The interlude with the Metropolitan Opera was well and truly over; there would be no more musical theatre engagements. No more opera – never again. No opera directorship, no director's office where banalities piled up on his desk all the way to the ceiling, where people might knock, scratch, hammer at the door at any time of the day or night, and where singers behaved like infants, screaming, crying and stamping their feet on the parquet. From now on there would be nothing but music.

He had built up his strength over the summer; now he worked from early morning until late at night, if not with the whole orchestra, then at least with small groups of instruments: strings first thing in the morning, woodwind before noon, percussion at midday, brass in the afternoon and the rest in the evening.

Sometimes he would pluck out a musician to go over a particular passage, or even the whole piece, with him. During a rehearsal for the *Eroica*, he made a young hornist play his part solo in front of the entire orchestra. He interrupted, made him start again from the beginning, interrupted over and over again, and kept doing so until the piece was more or less right and tears of shame and exertion were running down the horn player's scarlet cheeks.

Perhaps it was the energy born of resistance, a sort of stubborn fury, that drove the orchestra to its limits and beyond. He had experienced it many times before: despair, defiance, breakdown, then, ultimately, breakthrough and resolution. If, that is, the fury and the energy were great enough. If they weren't, things got stuck at despair. Even then, though, they had to keep going. And breakthroughs were only brief respites, a pause for breath along the way.

His place was at the conductor's stand. He had found it on one of his first days as orchestra director, in the basement storage room of the Court Opera, between a papier-mâché Roman column and a heap of moth-holed fabric panels. It was an old, rickety, worm-eaten wooden frame with a carelessly screwed-on desk, but it was precisely this unmysterious functionality that pleased him. He had wiped off the dust with a soft cloth and carried it up himself to the orchestra pit, where it served him modestly and well for the whole of his tenure. When he resigned the directorship ten years later, he was firmly convinced that it was this stand more than anything that had helped him to overcome the spite of the Viennese and emerge essentially unscathed, so he had it sent on to New York, in the teeth of Alma's vigorous resistance. She hated it for 'aesthetic reasons', and had suggested at least once every winter that they chop it up and use it as firewood. As soon as he stood behind it, he felt safer and more secure than anywhere else in the world. The stand had witnessed his growth to maturity as a conductor. As a young man, he was all movement; the papers had caricatured him as a jack-in-the-box, a Jewish monkey. They diagnosed him with St Vitus' Dance and compared him to someone who was mentally ill, possessed by a dybbuk, making grotesque movements with no apparent logical shape. As he got older, though, he grew calmer, his movements more economical. Nowadays he stood almost motionless, apart from his right hand drawing delicate lines in the air, and his eyes, which were said to light up sometimes during concerts like glowing coals, and reflected the electric lights in the auditorium like tiny flashes of lightning during the applause.

Sometimes he thought of his stand with a furtive tenderness, as if it were a living creature. It's as forbearing as an old donkey, he thought. It has experienced and endured a lot. The worms and the dust. The ink and the sweat. All those blows with the baton and the open palm. It has absorbed a life's worth of anger and delight.

The sun was high now, and the brightness of the sky hurt his eyes. A great white bird was perched on the railing about ten metres away. Its long tail fanned across the deck like a bridal veil. As it raised its wings and disappeared, silent as a shadow, Mahler felt a jolt in his chest and gave a quiet groan. He had been asleep, and he knew that it was fear.

His feet were cold, but his face was burning like fire. And yet he really didn't feel too bad. For a while now he had been hungry again, but he knew he wouldn't be able to keep anything down. They were probably still at breakfast two floors below. Anna was sure to be preoccupied with the marmalade. First she would stick her fingers in the glass jar, then, eyes closed, into her mouth. He should have got her a whole pot of this marmalade on the way over and slipped it into her little basket in New York. The thought of her delighted face made him strangely happy, and at the same time he knew it was too late, and was ashamed.

He rang for the boy, and moments later heard the quick steps on the metal staircase. He must have been waiting down there. Presumably they had assigned him to be permanently on hand. Mahler wondered what the boy thought of him. He caught himself hoping that he liked him, but who knew; it didn't really matter, anyway.

'Perhaps you would like some more tea?' asked the boy. He had taken off his cap, and Mahler could see the blue of the sky in his eyes.

'Have you been sitting down there on the stairs all this time?' he asked.

'Not all the time,' said the boy.

'What have they told you about me?'

'They said you were famous. For your music. And that I should look after you. Make sure you don't get cold. That the tea isn't too hot. That sort of thing.'

'But the tea should be hot.'

'As you wish.'

'Incidentally, it's absolutely ridiculous that there's no Russian white tea on this ship.'

'I didn't know there was a tea like that. Is it good?'

'The best. It soothes the soul.'

'Then I'll get some as soon as we dock,' said the boy. 'And next time you travel with us, I'll serve you a cup of white Russian tea every day.'

'That's very thoughtful of you,' said Mahler. 'I believe you'll go far.'

'I don't know if that's what I want. People who go far take longer to get there.'

'Where did you hear that?'

'No idea,' said the boy, and shrugged. 'I think I thought of it myself.'

'Just now?'

'Yes,' said the boy. 'Would you like me to bring you another blanket?'

'No, I'm perfectly warm,' said Mahler. 'I'd like you to tell me about the sea.'

'I don't know much about it yet. Only that it's no fun – that I know for sure. Sometimes there are storms that appear out of nowhere, and suddenly the sky's black and there are waves that will take a man with them in the blink of an eye if he doesn't attach himself. You need to know what you're doing then. But it's not just the waves and the storms. It's the weather generally. You practically burn up during the day, especially in uniform. And at night it's often icy cold. I heard of two men who froze to death on deck duty. They fell asleep, and when they were found after their shift they were sitting there back to back, stiff as boards, with their faces turned up to the sky. Maybe the stars were the last things they ever saw.'

The boy fell silent for a moment, then he said, 'Something like that wouldn't happen to me. I know exactly what I need to do. I've never been very interested in stars, either. Or the navigational tables; they're just numbers you have to learn by heart. I prefer the sun.'

'The sun is a star as well,' said Mahler.

'Of course,' said the boy. 'But you don't freeze to death when it shines.'

Mahler pushed himself forward and groped for the cushions supporting his back. He wheezed and struggled to breathe, but the boy was beside him, and he let him take him by the shoulders and raise him up, as lightly as if he were made of cork. The boy stuffed the cushions behind him and Mahler sat upright, gazing out over the sea.

'When I was your age, I never thought I'd see the sea. Now I've seen it so often, and I still don't really have a sense of it. I know more about mountains. Have you ever been to the mountains?'

'No,' said the boy. 'They're supposed to be beautiful. Is it true the peaks are always white?'

'Some of them, yes.'

'I wonder whether you can freeze to death up there as easily as you can at sea.'

'Sometimes they find bodies in the ice that look as fresh after forty years as if they'd set out yesterday.'

'I saw a body in the water once, in Cherbourg. A man. They dragged him out of the dock with long poles. His belly had blown up like a balloon, and the fish had eaten his face.'

Mahler glanced at the boy. His small, childlike mouth had grimaced at the memory of the body in the dock. His uniform and cap were spotlessly white. His patent leather shoes shone in the sun. He probably polished them every morning before sunrise, with the shoe-cleaning kit he had stowed under his bed in the sleeping quarters he shared with the other men, where it smelled of iron and sweat and the machines roared next door.

'Mr Director,' said the boy.

'Yes,' said Mahler. He had half-closed his eyes and was listening to the pounding of the engines.

'What kind of music do you make? Will you tell me something about it?'

'No. You can't talk about music; there's no language for it. As soon as music can be described, it's bad.'

The boy looked at him with big, shining eyes.

'I think I'll go now,' he said. 'Shall I bring you another pot of tea?'

Mahler shook his head.

'Make sure you stay warm,' said the boy. 'Mind your feet, especially.'

'Yes,' said Mahler. 'Have they told you that I'm dying?'

'No,' said the boy, and Mahler could see it was a lie.

'Tell my wife I'd like to be alone a little longer. They should get ready in about an hour. I'll ring the bell.'

'I'll let them know. Take care of yourself, Mr Director.'

The boy left. Mahler loosened the blanket and stretched out his legs. All that talking had exhausted him. He would have liked to sleep, but he was afraid of sleep. He closed his eyes and thought of Alma and the child. He tried to picture Anna's face, but something different came to mind, an image of sadness and pain.

In early November, the day before the first concert of the season – Beethoven, Liszt and Strauss – he had walked back to the hotel after the dress rehearsal through the rainy New York streets. As always, he took a detour through the park, walking beneath the trees in the cold, damp air, looking forward to the warm hotel room and a few quiet hours with his family. The lights of the Savoy shone out at him from afar, and when he entered the foyer, filled with the buzz of hotel guests' voices, he felt at home for the first time in a long while.

Anna was sitting on the floor in a corner of their room, so engrossed in her game that she didn't notice him at all. Mahler stopped and observed his daughter. She had wrapped two dolls in a cloth and placed them in a large fruit bowl. She sat beside them, brushing and smoothing their hair. Her movements were angular and childlike, but her eyes held a tender expression she had copied from her mother. When she noticed him, she cried out in surprise and threw herself into his arms. They rolled on the carpet, laughing, then lay side by side on their backs. He stroked her hair, and his hand rested for a moment against her soft, warm cheek.

'Do the dolls have to go to bed already?'

'Yes, Papa. They've had an exhausting day. Just like you.'

'I'm sure their day was much more exhausting than mine, am I right?' he said, turning his head to the bedroom door, where Alma was standing, smiling down at him.

'I'm sure it was,' she said. 'After all, you're a thoroughly lazy and dissolute man.'

'Yes,' he said, jumping up from the floor. 'And I can be even more dissolute!'

'I know,' she said. 'But not until after dinner.'

Alma had set the table. She did this once a week, when the maid had her day off, or when she simply felt like it. She had spread out a plain tablecloth and put a white hyacinth in the middle of the table. He was sure they would be having potato soup and bread. He had smelled it as soon as he came in, and was looking forward to the hot soup. When he sat down, he saw that the table was set for four.

'Are we expecting someone?' he asked.

'We're not expecting anyone,' she said. 'Today's the third of November. Maria's birthday. She would have been seven today.'

Mahler looked at the fourth place setting. He nodded, then stretched out his hand as if to grasp something; but there was nothing there, and he dropped it again.

Since then, two years had passed. It was four years since Maria's death, but it seemed to him that he could hear her voice beneath the stamping of the ship's engines and the slapping of the waves. The cough and rattle of her last breaths.

He opened his eyes and looked up at the sky, where there was now a single, translucent, feathery cloud. It's all alone up there, he thought. It'll disappear before it's even grown into a proper storm cloud. He thought it would be nice if it rained. He would have a canopy of resin-coated sailcloth erected over his spot, then he could stay sheltered and dry and gaze out over the seething ocean.

'You won't be able to hold yourself together,' he said, 'frail and bedraggled as you are.'

He gave a short laugh, but immediately felt a stabbing pain in his chest, and something within him clenched. So this is what it's come to, he thought. Just before the end, I've started talking to clouds.

He closed his eyes again. He longed for Alma's hand on his chest, on the spot where he had felt the pain. He loved her hands, perhaps more than anything. When they were still living in Vienna, he would sometimes drive out to the Vienna Woods with her, just to be able to hold her hand away from prying eyes; and when he was alone in a train carriage during a concert tour, or sitting in a hotel room that smelled of dust and petroleum, he would picture her hands before he thought of her face.

They had met almost exactly four years after he was appointed director of the Court Opera, and for a long time his love for her had consumed him. There were nights when he had walked the streets for hours, overcome with longing, and when at last they met again the following morning, in a coffee house or in the Stadtpark, he greeted her with a child's expression of radiant wonder.

It had started very simply. They were introduced at a Viennese soirée. She was sitting at the table and he couldn't stop looking at her. He had already heard about her: that she was a beautiful, really quite splendid young woman from a very good family, clever, confident, a little talkative perhaps, certainly somewhat exhausting, but this was the woman half of Vienna was currently mad about, a woman who could pick her men like currants from the cake of society. And now here she was, fiddling with the wax on one of the white candles and chatting to an elderly gentleman. She was even more beautiful than he had imagined. She was tall and voluptuous, and her movements were both soft and awkward, like those of a dancing child. Sometimes, when she laughed, she threw back her head, and he saw her neck, which was as white and smooth as marble.

After the meal the guests settled in little groups, and he went to sit with her. There was tea and cake, and she flicked a crumb from the collar of his jacket; he couldn't help laughing at the audacity of her touch, but it also secretly alarmed him. They talked about music, and as he listened to her words he gazed into her eyes, which seemed to him unusually dark. When he took his leave, he kissed her hand. Her fingers were cold, as if they had been bathed in ice.

They saw each other frequently: he invited her to the opera, and felt her eyes on him as he conducted rehearsals for *The Tales of Hoffmann*. He told her that he had resolved to play every single note Beethoven had ever committed to paper. This, however, was the last thing he would demand of himself; you couldn't expect much more from an opera house like this, although when he took up the post it had been in order to give music the space it deserved, which was far above and beyond the parochial conceptions of the supposed Viennese aesthetic sensibility, a sensibility that was really just small-minded, even coarse and provincial – a plan that had of course been attacked, undermined, ignored or simply overlooked by this small-mindedness or coarseness from the very beginning. In spite of this, he had found ways and means to push the Court Opera and its employees to the limits of their capacity for inner growth. The ways, of course, were difficult, the means constrained, so, as one could imagine, something like this was not achieved easily or without resistance; there had been much wailing and gnashing of teeth. But this ongoing struggle, working tirelessly to overcome such resistance, was the only potentially successful way of making music. Anything else was just a clanging and scraping that stuffed people's ears and minds with increasingly invasive, ever-expanding accumulations of sound. Furthermore, most musicians – or, as the case may be, players of musical works – imagined that they and they alone were capable of bringing music to life. Of course, this was, firstly, an expression of unbridled hubris, and, secondly, utter nonsense, since music itself transcended all imagination *a priori*. Music surpassed all human beings, and essentially needed neither musicians nor an audience. Music needed nothing and nobody: it was simply there.

All this he said to Alma without even knowing why; after all, it didn't really matter. The only thing that did was that she sat, stood or walked beside him while he talked, close enough for him to be able to smell her. He had the impression that her hair (or skin, he couldn't yet tell) had a slight scent of fir tree resin, which he told her. She laughed, and he took her in his arms and kissed her.

Four months lay between the evening of the cake crumb and the wedding. He arrived on foot and in galoshes. It was pouring with rain; the drains could not contain the deluge of water, and Mahler had to dodge puddles and jump over rivulets. Outside St Charles's Church sat a beggar, leaning against one of the portal columns with his few possessions, a hat and a pile of old newspapers spread out in front of him. Mahler had often seen him before, on his way to the Opera House, or when he went for a walk between rehearsals. He was a small, gaunt man of indeterminate age; his face was covered in blisters, crusts and skin tags, and his hands were wrapped in tattered rags with only the tips of his fingers showing. He used to shuffle about the square and around the church, always bent over with his eyes fixed on the ground, sometimes picking things up and slipping them into one of his coat pockets. In summer he would also be seen in the Stadtpark, sitting on a bench with his ravaged face turned up towards the sun until it bloomed crimson.

'You don't look like a bridegroom,' he said, as Mahler came running up the steps.

'How do you know I am one, then?' Mahler asked.

'I don't,' the beggar replied. 'I just said you don't look like one, that's all.'

Mahler tossed a few coins into his hat and stepped through the portal. Everyone was already waiting at the altar: Alma, her mother, her stepfather, Mahler's sister Justine and her husband, and the priest. Seven people in that cold, high-ceilinged space. Mahler's steps echoed beneath the church roof as he hurried forward.

Later, whenever he tried to picture the moments just before their marriage, for some reason it was not Alma's face he saw but that of the beggar at the door. He couldn't remember what Alma's stepfather had wanted when he leant towards him and whispered urgently in his ear, and he couldn't recall a single word the priest had said, but he could still hear himself say 'Yes', the word, to his surprise, coming out loud and clear.

Two days later, the newlyweds boarded a train for St Petersburg, where Mahler had been invited to conduct three concerts of Haydn, Schubert and Beethoven in the Hall of the Nobles. On the third evening of their journey, while they were at dinner in the restaurant car, he put down his knife and fork, pressed the balls of his hands against his temples and slowly slid under the opulent table laden with fruit and cold cuts. It was the migraine: yet again he spent hours lying flat on the ground with all his limbs outstretched, on the ribbed wooden floor of his compartment this time, staring in silent horror at the flickering apparitions that swarmed around the pain in his head.

They spent three weeks in St Petersburg, and while they enjoyed their visits to the Hermitage and the many palaces and churches, the forays into magnificently illuminated shops and the walks on the frozen Neva that glittered in the light of innumerable torches, Mahler was secretly shocked by the destitution that surrounded them in the darkness amidst the splendour, and yearned for the narrow, unspectacular streets of downtown Vienna.

Later, though, it was another image entirely that kept returning to him, one that touched him most of all. It was early evening and snowing heavily as he was coming home from an orchestra rehearsal. Alma was sitting at a table in the window of the café in the foyer of the Hotel d'Angleterre. She was alone, a bottle of red wine in front of her; her hand was playing with the glass, and she had barely taken a sip from it. From a distance she was as beautiful as ever, but as he drew closer and was able to make out her eyes, he saw that they were clouded. Her gaze was empty; she seemed to be staring into a nothingness beyond the snowstorm on the street. All of a sudden she noticed him and raised her hand to wave. The gesture was tired and feeble, and she let the hand fall.

This was the image that stayed with him for the rest of his life: his beautiful young wife, alone and terribly tired, in the brightly lit window of the Russian hotel café.

In his first season as a married man he conducted fifty-four performances and some one hundred rehearsals; in addition, there was the administration, press, personnel, politics. The Opera in spring, autumn and winter; in summer, composition by the lake. As a conductor and opera house director, he never had more power. He was married to the most beautiful woman in Vienna; everyone loved him, while some revered him and wanted to be around him, to touch him, shake his hand, embrace him. When he had to, he let them. When he could, he ran away. The director is in a hurry, has just left, is off out again. From his desk to rehearsals, the basement, the foyer, parliament, the Court, and back again. Non-stop rushing and racing about. And everywhere resistance. Not all traditions – which were really no more than the expression of a steadfast determination to remain eternally the same, lifeless and dull – could simply be swept aside. Time-honoured customs had powerful guardians, and they were everywhere: in the porter's lodge, the subscription office, the prompt box and the orchestra pit, in the offices of bureaucrats and lawyers, in the city hall, at the newspaper editor's desk. Everywhere people were talking. Were upset and confused. Had a bad feeling. Were just expressing an opinion. All those trips the director went on, for example: Berlin, Munich, Amsterdam, Strasbourg, Breslau, Trieste and so on. All over the map. As if Vienna weren't big enough, and the Vienna Court Opera just some rickety village bandstand. And what were they supposed to make of it when someone showed up and started to retouch Beethoven's Ninth? A Jew who cuts down and paints over the greatest work in the German musical canon, just because he feels like it? And then resolutely insists on staging *Salome*, a stomach-turning piece of third-rate smut?

A Jew, of all people, who drives the Court Opera into deficit, dipping his fingers into the already half-empty pockets of the Viennese? It would be laughable, of course, if it weren't profoundly sad, and enough to drive a man to despair. But that's just how it is: you'll always be what you are, you'll never get to be anyone else. Not even the most beautiful woman in Vienna or the most affecting *Fidelio* will make any difference. Nothing in this world lasts for ever. Nothing under the sun remains unseen.

In May 1907 he tendered his resignation. The Kaiser issued a decree to this effect and approved his requests for a payoff and a widow's and orphan's pension for the children. The American engagement was already fixed, the contracts with the Metropolitan Opera signed, the voyage booked. Before that, he and his family would go to the lake once more, for a carefree, idle summer. As the train pulled out of Vienna West station, he sank back in his upholstered seat. For a while he sat there, pale and silent, then he began to laugh. He laughed until the tears came to his eyes and his voice cracked, and he didn't stop until the train reached Purkersdorf in the Vienna Woods. Just then, he felt more tired and empty than ever before in his life, yet he also had the peculiar sense that he could go on like this for a very long time. As if this were another chance at life.

That was two weeks before Maria died, and when he boarded the *Kaiserin Auguste Victoria* that winter to cross the Atlantic to New York, he couldn't bring himself to look back even once.

In vain he tried to recall details of that first voyage; he could barely summon a single clear image. All he remembered was the wind and the icy cold. Once, he stood on deck all night without hat or gloves, staring out into the roaring darkness illuminated only here and there by vague glints of light. When two officer cadets came across him shortly before dawn, shook him out of his paralysis, wrapped him in blankets and took him to his cabin, he merely registered it with quiet surprise.

'We've still got a long way to go, haven't we?' he asked, as they laid him on his bed and took off his shoes.

'A long way, Mr Director, sir.'

He held out his stiff, frozen hand to them, thanked them and fell asleep.

That was all. Everything else was confused. The floating particles of his memory swirled about, re-assembling only slowly into an image of New York harbour, where once again he was standing on deck, next to Alma this time, holding little Anna's hand and watching a gang of dock workers with blackened faces dismantle wooden scaffolding with saws and axes amidst noisy shouts and laughter.

Sitting on the sundeck, Mahler contemplated the meaninglessness of life with a twinge of baleful resignation. Life was little more than a brief exhalation, a breath in the storm of the world, yet he loved it so much that his sadness at the futility of this love almost broke his heart.

'It could all have gone quite differently. We should have swum across to the other shore. It was a mistake to turn back halfway. Who does such a thing?'

Mahler spoke into the wind. His head jerked up, and he blinked in the bright sunlight. He hadn't slept enough these past few weeks, and it felt as if the tiredness and pain were sinking deeper and deeper into his bones. I shouldn't complain, he thought. I'm tired, but so are others. And the pain has been worse.

The cloud had vanished; the sky was white and empty. Mahler leant against the steel wall at an angle and tried to bear it. He could hear voices again on the lower deck. People were talking over each other;

someone laughed, and then it was quiet again, apart from the wind and the sound of the sea.

Tears suddenly sprang to his eyes and he sobbed into his palms. He thought of the others, their faces and voices, and his guilt.

'I would so have liked to live longer,' he said out loud.

This made him feel ridiculous, and he was embarrassed. The sun is up there, he thought. As long as you can still see it, it's not over. Come on, walk towards it, a few steps at least. Get up. Move about. It's good for the bones, and it won't do your heart any harm, either.

He bent forward and started unwrapping the blanket from around his legs, which was trickier than he had anticipated. The boy had done a good job: his legs were packaged like the bales of Cuban tobacco he had watched being loaded into the temperature-controlled cargo bays of the *Kaiserin Auguste Victoria* in New York.

He was starting to get hot; he tugged at the blanket with both hands, and felt sweat trickle down his back. He sat up, dangled his legs over the edge of the chest and inched forward until the tips of his toes touched the ground. He let himself slip over the edge, and was briefly astonished to find himself standing.

It would be easier if I had my walking stick, he thought. Why did I leave it in the cabin? He had had it made in Toblach by the same carpenter who had been so negligent when putting up the fly screens. He had found the stick himself, in the forest; all the man had to do was strip the bark, sand it down, immerse it in an oil bath and fit it with a horn handle. And this time he had done a good job. The stick sat pleasantly slim and heavy in the hand, and the knots looked like little faces peering open-mouthed from the wood. He always took it on his travels and on hiking trips; not that he really needed it, he just liked to have it with him. I could do with you now, he thought. But you're hanging downstairs in the cloakroom, and I have no idea whether I'll ever hold you in my hand again.

Stop thinking about the stick, he thought. Think about yourself. Go slowly. Pay attention. That's it. He steadied himself with one hand on the edge of the container, then let go and shuffled jerkily forward. The railing was about two metres away; when he had covered half the distance, he let himself fall, grabbed the handrail with both hands and leant into the wind. In the shadow of the ship he could clearly see the streaks of brown and green seaweed drifting sluggishly astern.

It's full of life down there, he thought. Quite

unlike the heavens. Up above, it's all empty and dead. Strange, really, for people to hope that's where they'll go. Then he thought again of Alma and their little daughter. Had they finished breakfast yet? What time was it, actually? The sun was high; how much higher did it get in April? Of course they would have finished, ages ago. Alma had left the little one with the maid and was lying in bed. She wasn't asleep. She was lying there with her eyes open, watching the reflection of the waves on the ceiling. One hand on her stomach, the other on the pillow by her head, fingers playing with the silken material. What will you do? he wondered. You're a strong woman. Not as strong as you think, but strong enough. There'll be enough money. Who knows what is to come.

A tremor passed through his body. His legs ached, and he could feel their strength draining away. Alma had often made fun of his legs; stalks, she called them, which was exactly what they were.

He tried to take the strain off one leg by shifting his weight, but he immediately felt a searing pain in his back and stopped.

'Just shiver, old man,' he said. 'Shivering keeps you warm.'

He would hold on. He had enough strength in his arms, and his fingers were firmly clamped around the handrail. He could stand like this for a long time.

It seemed to him that the seaweed was slipping past more quickly now, but it could be his imagination. Nothing was certain. He thought about the lake. Sometimes, when the children were having their siesta, he used to swim out alone. He would stop in the middle of the lake and dive down. The water was cloudy in summer, and you couldn't see more than a few metres. He kept his eyes shut and let himself drift underwater, where he could hear the sounds of the lake: the gentle murmur of the currents, the whisper of the wind stroking the surface and, sometimes, a dull, mysterious boom that startled him and sounded like a distant explosion.

The sky seemed to be clouding over in the west. Grey mist rose up and darkened the horizon. When was the last time it had rained? He couldn't remember. Rain will do me good, he thought. A man needs fresh water. Salt corrodes the lungs.

I shouldn't worry about a thing like that, he thought. There's no more time.

He thought back to the previous summer. On the way to Toblach he had grabbed Alma by the arm to confront her. She looked at him, and a shadow flitted across her forehead, although the day was hot and cloudless.

'It's not true,' he said.

'Let go,' she said. 'You're hurting me.'

He let her go, and for a moment they stood facing each other in silence.

'It's not true,' he said again.

'Stop it. I've told you everything.'

'No, you haven't. I read the letter.'

'It's just words on a piece of paper. People always read what they want to read. Why did you have to read it, anyway? It was my letter. You should have kept your hands off it.'

'It was addressed to me.'

'By mistake. You know that.'

'Your architect is an idiot. You're the lover of an idiot.'

'I'm not his lover.'

'What are you, then?'

'I am what you could see if you ever really looked at me properly.'

Her dark eyes were very wide. There was an expression in them that he had only ever seen once before, and it frightened him.

'Do you think I like being like this?' he said. 'I don't recognise myself any more. But maybe I'm just imagining it, and I've never really known myself at all. I'm jealous. I hate you. And I love you. You're my light.'

'My God, you're so dramatic.'

'I only ask one thing. Don't lie to me any more. Tell me about him. Tell me who he is.'

'He's a person. He moves and speaks. He breathes. He has a little hollow in the muscles of his arm, just above the elbow. I haven't worked out what it is, and I haven't yet dared to ask.'

'You bitch!' he said.

'What do you expect? Everything I once believed in has ceased to exist. Maybe it was never there. They did warn me. All he thinks about is his music. He's old. He's got St Vitus' Dance. The Jewish malady. He chews on his conscience in the lining of his cheeks. Look at him. It's his ancestry that's to blame. But I didn't listen to them. I wanted you: you were Gustav Mahler, the genius, and I fell in love with you. With your hands. Your mouth. Your ridiculously high forehead. It was a dream, and we dreamed it together for a while. But now I've woken up.'

For an instant he thought he couldn't bear it any longer. Everything in him tensed up. He wanted to run away, and saw himself running down the road to the other side of the valley and on into the black and silent forest.

'And the children?' he said finally. 'Did we just dream them as well?'

'One of them is dead.'

'What are you saying?'

'I'm saying that one of our children is dead. That's all.'

Mahler looked into her sad, angry face. He thought of Maria. He saw her lying on the bed, as if turned to stone, the wound on her neck covered by a silk scarf; her hands were folded on her stomach and as white as snow. He couldn't picture her face. There was nothing now where once her face had been.

'Will you see him again?' he asked abruptly.

'What if I did?' she said. 'I'm a woman. He's a man. It's that simple. Of course, you have no clue about that. A genius doesn't concern himself with such things. He doesn't want to think about them when all he ever does is strive to reach the highest pinnacle. But there is no highest pinnacle. There's always something higher. I know what you're going to say. But I can't hear it any more. I've had enough. Your moods. Your illnesses. The way you behave in company. Your temper tantrums, your jealousy, your boundless egotism. I fell in love with a child, but a woman needs more than a child by her side!'

'He's an architect.'

'He's a man. And I'm not going to explain to you in detail what exactly makes him a man. He loves me; he wants to spend his life with me. He's serious. His eyes are gentle and sad, even when he laughs, and he laughs a lot. He moves me. Do you know how that feels? It's like a whole new life.'

'There's only this one life.'

'Yes, that's probably true. Which is why I'm going to live it exactly as I wish. I was always a good wife to you. That's what they say, isn't it? *A good wife.* I supported you. I believed in you. In your music, and all the fascination around it. I waited for you: at home, at the theatre, in hotel rooms. All I ever did was wait.'

'You're usually drunk when I get home.'

'I drink a glass or two in the evening. More, if need be. Because otherwise life would be unbearably empty and tedious. Do you remember your promises? The house with the blue door and the three pianos, one just for me? The meadow with the raspberry bushes? The drives in an open-topped car?'

Again he saw the expression he had seen before, and as if in a distorting mirror saw his own consternation in her face.

'Forgive me,' he said. He abruptly thudded to his knees and clasped her hips in his hands. 'Please, please forgive me!'

Alma's whole body trembled. She put a hand on his head, and at the same time made a feeble attempt to pull away.

'Get up,' she said. 'Please, get up!'

Mahler pressed his face to her belly. Then, slowly and with difficulty, he unclenched the fingers he had dug into her skirt and got to his feet.

The landscape quivered in the midday heat. Skylarks whirred over the fields, and away in the distance cows stood out tiny and brown against the dark green of the wooded hills.

'I'm sorry,' said Alma, looking down at the patch of grass where he had knelt. 'I think I should go now,' she said, wearily. 'I'm melting in this heat.'

'Don't go,' he said. 'Please, don't go.'

'It'd be easier, really. I'm exhausted. I can't think any more, and it's all so painful.'

'Why don't we walk to the little forest lake? The path is shady; we could hire a horse and cart, if you like. I can't remember the two of us ever going swimming on our own. It's quiet up there. The water is nice and cool. And there are rainbow dragonflies. You've always liked dragonflies.'

She shook her head, and he saw that she was crying.

'I love you,' he said.

She said nothing, just went on shaking her head, then raised her hand and placed the back of it against her forehead. For a moment she stayed like that, as if she had to ward something off, then she turned and left. He watched her walk back along the path to the farmhouse until she plunged into the shadow of the apricot trees, their boughs weighed down with fruit, before finally disappearing behind the building.

Gustav Mahler stood at the railing, leaning into the wind at an angle, and tried to remember what had happened next. But it was as if his memories of the remaining hours of that hot summer day had dissolved along with Alma's shape beneath the fruit trees. Back then she had left, and for a moment it seemed utterly incomprehensible, almost unreal, that she was still here. That she was sitting a few floors down from him right now, perhaps even thinking of him, or at least thinking of preparing some bread and marmalade for him and sending it up.

His illness was probably what had held her back. His begging and pleading, his threats and promises, the ridicule he had exposed himself to, the humiliations he inflicted on himself – none of this would have been enough to stop Alma from leaving. Only the prospect of impending death had been able to do that.

She had been right. He hadn't seen her. He had looked at her as you might contemplate a vase. Or one of those white seed heads that blow across the fields in early summer; sometimes one would find its way into the composing hut and sit, quivering, on the piano for a while before being caught by a draught of air and borne out of the window. Even now, if he closed his eyes, he couldn't picture her clearly. She had become a blur: sometimes it seemed to him that he was simply dreaming her. He loved her, but what did that love still mean? What did it mean that she had stayed with him? Did she choose him? Or did she just want to ease an old man's death?

Hysterical, he thought. Hysterical, like a little girl. Pull yourself together. It was quite simple. A man dies. A woman lives. That was all there was to say. What she did with her life was no longer any of his business. She would stay with him until the end; that was more than he had a right to expect. He was the one who was leaving, after all. For a while he had cherished the illusion that she would forget his rival. Even if she did, though, it would soon be the next one's turn. All that is transitory is but a likeness. It was enough to make you weep.

He found himself thinking of the chaos that had ensued in the weeks that followed. All the conversations, the breakdowns, the weeping at the kitchen table, the terrible dreams, the nights when he had stood beside her bed like a ghost and watched her sleeping. How his yearning for her body, for a look from her, a single touch, had intensified to the point of madness. And finally: the architect, who had had the audacity to show up in Toblach. One day there he was, standing slim and grey beneath the little bridge by the meadow. He looked less German than Mahler had imagined. An ordinary young man in a double-breasted suit and a hat that was much too big for him. Mahler took him up to the farmhouse, and while Alma and the architect talked in the kitchen he knelt on the floor two rooms away and beseeched God for help, the God he had scarcely even thought of in years.

He never learned what was said between them in the kitchen. Half an hour later they emerged, stony-faced and white as a sheet, like a pair of horror-struck siblings. The architect departed, and as Mahler stared after the train from the window of his composing hut, clouds of white steam blanketing the flower-filled slopes, for the briefest of moments he felt he had been saved.

That, of course, was nonsense. The other man had gone for now, but his slim figure still seemed to cast a shadow that darkened the whole of the valley, right up to the karstic peaks.

Towards the end of August, Mahler developed tonsillitis. He had caught a harmless cold from Anna that quickly turned into a nasty throat infection. One night he awoke with a fever, suddenly convinced that he was the last living creature in the house, probably the whole region. He lay in the darkness feeling more desolate and alone than ever before in his life. When the moon appeared in his window around midnight, he saw the big white bird for the first time in the tree outside. He was seized by dizziness. The bed seemed to be slowly swaying, and he lay there digging both hands into the mattress to steady himself. The bird sat in the moonlight, dazzling white and motionless. Its feathers billowed once as if caught by a gust of wind. Mahler swung round, groped in the bedside cabinet for a candle and lit it. He froze as his own shadow flickered into life on the ceiling above and seemed slowly to descend. He screamed, and as he stumbled from the room, out of the corner of his eye, he saw the bird turn its head.

Alma found him on the floor outside her bedroom. He was lying with his head on the threshold in the light of the candle, which was wedged into a crack in the floorboards and had almost burned down. He seemed to be asleep with his eyes open, and it was a while before he responded to Alma's calling and pleading.

'I'm burning up,' he said.

It wasn't his first attack of fever, but it was the first from which he didn't fully recover. He stayed in bed for three days and nights, and Alma fed him lukewarm soup with a teaspoon. Sometimes, especially in the early morning, he would put his head in her lap, whimpering softly as she patiently ran her fingers through his hair.

On the fourth day he felt better. He spurned the soup and demanded fresh bread and milky coffee.

After breakfast he put on his best summer suit, said goodbye to Alma and the little one and set off for Holland to meet Professor Sigmund Freud.

Now, less than a year later, he recalled this journey as an experience from a different time. Squinting into the wind, which had begun to blow in cold, capricious gusts, he tried to remember the advice the professor had given him. He had thought of contacting Freud during his time in Vienna, but his motive then had been a more general interest in psychoanalysis, its fabled possibilities and aberrations. Now, everything was at stake.

They had telegraphed back and forth a few times, and eventually the professor had invited him to come to the small town of Leiden, where he was holidaying with his family. The two-day journey had given Mahler plenty of time to consider how to articulate his predicament.

They sat in a café and drank hot lemonade with honey, then went for a walk along the Rapenburg Canal. Mahler remembered the oily, bottle-green water, pitch black under the bridges and in the shadow of the boats. It was the height of summer, but the place already smelled of autumn, putrid and damp. It was enjoyable to walk beside the professor. Freud had no difficulty keeping up with him. He took short, quick steps, holding one hand at his back and, in the other, the stump of a cigar that reeked of dry manure; its feeble glow had to be repeatedly relit. Mahler was surprised by how young he looked. He had secretly expected to find a withered, almost doddery old man, but Freud was full of vigour. A man in his prime.

What had he told the professor? He had talked about loneliness, and about his mother. The mother was obvious. But why loneliness? He had been alone for half his life, but he had never felt lonely. Even now, when a part of Alma's soul had flown towards the architect, he didn't feel lonely. He felt sick. Wounded. Desperate. But not lonely. In this respect he really was a child. Loneliness was a feeling only adults could cope with. A person who felt lonely still had the ability to focus on himself. The self was, as it were, the centre of his world. Mahler, however, had never reached this stage. He had never outgrown the childish terror of abandonment. In some ways he was still standing there, forsaken, bound by a cruel spell that compelled him to watch over and over again, in his mind's eye, the person he loved more than anything in the world dissolve in the shadow of an apricot tree.

'Don't talk nonsense,' Freud had said. 'Nobody dissolves like that. It may have been a bit destabilising for your personhood. In all other respects you're fit as a fiddle and, above all, not a child any more.'

The walk lasted less than four hours. Afterwards, the two men shook hands and bade each other farewell.

'I'm going inside now, into the warm,' the professor said. 'It gets uncomfortable outdoors in the evening. The countryside here is flat. The wind comes in off the sea and brings the cold with it.'

'And the damp,' said Mahler.

'It's such a beautiful country, though.'

'Yes. Very beautiful.'

'How long will you be on the train?'

'Two days,' said Mahler. 'One and a half, if all goes smoothly. At least I can work.'

'Yes – you can work,' said Freud. 'Send my regards to the mountains.'

'I will. What do I owe you?'

'You figure it out.'

'Understood. It was a pleasure to meet you.'

'The pleasure was all mine,' said Freud. 'Get yourself a jersey. Those carriages are draughty, especially the window seats.'

It's that simple, then, thought Mahler the next day, sitting in the train as it raced south across the Dutch lowlands. Work, and a warm jersey. What had he expected? A single conversation with a stranger wasn't going to mend his shattered heart. What had the professor said? Had he said anything at all, other than that thing about his mother and a few platitudes towards the end? Basically, Mahler had done all the talking. He had travelled more than a thousand kilometres, sleepless, with an inflamed and burning throat, just to walk along a canal, stare into the water and give a four-hour monologue.

There is no help, he thought. And there is no consolation. We are alone in the world.

Strangely, he didn't find the thought upsetting. Perhaps in the lack of consolation there was also something like the happiness of relief. Transitory, of course, but still.

Mahler shivered. Freud had been right. There was an icy draught in the carriage, as there had been on the outward journey. And he was tired. Dutch hotel beds were tiny, even by his standards; he had hardly slept, and his fever had returned. He leant his head against the window and stared out. The countryside lay in the early morning light, the wide white sky even emptier than the harvested fields stretching all the way to the horizon. There are no birds any more, and no clouds, he thought, and fell asleep.

'Your wife is asking after your health. She urges you to come down into the warm.'

Mahler hadn't heard the boy approach. He wasn't wearing a cap; his thin hair was ruffled by the wind, his mouth hung open, and he looked even more child-like than usual.

Who puts you to bed at night? Mahler thought. Who puts their hand on your forehead in the morning and whispers in your ear to wake you up?

'Did you tiptoe up on me?' he asked. 'You shouldn't do that. I want to hear you coming. I don't like surprises.'

'Please excuse me. I walked the same as always.'

'Tell my wife I'm warm enough. She can wait.'

'She asks if you wouldn't like to eat. A little

something, at least. She says you need to line your stomach for the day.'

'Tell her I'm not hungry.'

'She says if you don't come of your own accord, she'll issue instructions.'

'What instructions?'

'I couldn't tell you. But your wife does seem very strong-minded, if you don't mind me saying so.'

'What gives you that impression?' asked Mahler.

'I don't know,' said the boy. 'There's something about her . . . I don't think I understand these things.'

'Nobody understands these things. Now go and tell her I'm staying here a while longer. I feel fine, I'm not cold, I'm not hungry, and I'll ring when I'm ready.'

The boy nodded.

'Now what?' asked Mahler. 'Didn't you hear me?'

The boy's face shone in the sun; his cap had left a white stripe on his forehead, just below the hairline. He stood with his eyes fixed on Mahler and didn't move.

'Didn't you hear me?' Mahler repeated. 'I want you to go!'

All of a sudden he was furious. With Alma, and the way she bossed him about; with his own weakness, and with every single person who was aware of it. He was furious, and at the same time he felt helpless and stupid in front of this boy, who stood stubbornly before him with his hands balled into pink fists and pressed against the seam of his trousers.

'If you send me away, I'll go,' said the boy. 'But you shouldn't be alone for too long. And you should sit down again. The metal heats up in the sun; it'll do you good.'

Mahler looked the boy straight in the face. He wanted to tell him to go to hell, to go and get on someone else's nerves, but he looked serious and sad, and Mahler's fury disappeared as quickly as it had come.

'You're right,' he said. 'I'll let it heat up a while longer, then I'll sit back down.'

'Promise?'

'Promise. Now go downstairs and tell them to come and fetch me in half an hour. Not a minute earlier.'

'I will,' said the boy. 'You can count on me, Mr Director, sir.'

Mahler stared straight out over the ocean. He loved a wide, open view. In his childhood home there had been just a few narrow windows, all of which overlooked the street. On the opposite side were the two houses belonging to the district court judge and a butcher's with a licence to serve alcohol. On slaughter days the wind blew the smell of blood up into the attic room where he sat at the piano, its pedals elongated with blocks of wood so he could reach them with his short, spindly legs. Years later, well into adulthood, he still heard the pigs' death squeals in his dreams. If he wanted to see far into the distance, he had to go out of the dusty little town, climb over a few fences and head out into the fields. He remembered how he had loved to walk over the harvested land, where exaltations of skylarks would flutter up from time to time and flit about for a while, high overhead, before dropping down and disappearing in the shadow of the clods of turned earth. He loved the solitude out there: the space around him seemed infinite, and the sound of the wind and the bright larksong compensated for the constant noise and shouting he was exposed to at school and with his brothers and sisters. He would wander the countryside for hours; sometimes night would start to climb over the horizon, and he would have to run in order to get home before dark.

Alma was wrong. He wasn't a child. That little boy at the piano and in the fields, the sad-eyed six-year-old in the photograph in their old Vienna apartment, no longer existed.

Mahler felt the *Amerika* shudder beneath his feet. The handrail vibrated. The sea is alive, he thought. You just have to stand still long enough to feel it breathe.

He thought back to that first crossing, when he had stood on deck for hours staring into the distance; back then, though, he had not been wrapped in thick blankets or clutching the railing with cold fingers. The captain had told him that you were never alone at sea. Even if you were shipwrecked and clinging to a piece of driftwood in the middle of the Atlantic, there was more life around you than in all the cities of Europe and America put together, the man had said. Even the blackest and coldest depths were teeming with living organisms we couldn't even begin to imagine. How did he know this? Mahler had asked. After all, no one had been down there. The captain merely shrugged. A great many had been down there, he said; the trouble was that they were still lying there, with their skulls full of shells, and couldn't tell us anything. It was a bit like with God, he added: we didn't know anything about him either, but he undoubtedly existed, didn't he?

Back then, Mahler had found nothing comforting in the thought of floating over a dark realm populated by a host of curious living organisms, whether on a piece of driftwood or in the imperial cabin of a four-engined Norddeutscher Lloyd steamship. Now, though, the idea gave him something approaching quiet pleasure. Everything was full of life. Even death was a concept of the living. As long as you could still imagine it, it hadn't arrived.

But death had announced it was coming. Mahler remembered setting off for Munich in September the previous year to conduct the final rehearsals for the premiere of his Eighth Symphony. This time, he wore a woollen jersey and a scarf wrapped three times round his neck, and sat beside a window draped with heavy curtains to protect him from the draught. But as the train was passing the foothills of the Tyrolean Alps he began to shudder with cold, and perspiration poured down his burning face. On arrival in Munich he took a hackney carriage to the Hotel Continental, where he spent a whole day in bed trying to sweat out the fever under a thick layer of eiderdowns. Downstairs in the banqueting hall they were celebrating the birthday of some member of the local aristocracy, and the noise from the band travelled up the stairs and down the corridors. Mahler lay listening to the music, its wretched blaring and drumming, as he tried to make sense of his whirling thoughts, all of which revolved around the rehearsals and the upcoming concert.

The premiere of the Eighth Symphony was going to make history. That, at least, was the plan of the booking agent Emil Gutmann, who had organised the first performance of the Seventh in Munich a few years earlier – a successful, albeit rather modest, event with a relatively small orchestra. The success of that evening had sparked a desire in the impresario, who was furiously ambitious, to produce other, much bigger events. When he was entrusted with the direction of the music festival that was to be part of the Munich International Exhibition, he wanted it to conclude with Mahler's Eighth as its crowning glory. No other composition was sufficiently monumental to even begin to do justice to an enterprise on the huge scale Gutmann envisaged.

Months earlier, the biggest venue on the exhibition grounds had been converted into a concert hall of glass, steel and reinforced concrete, eclipsing everything that had gone before. The building was taller and wider than the *Kaiser Wilhelm II* or the *Amerika*, and when Mahler first stood in front of it, looking up at the floral arrangements that adorned the dizzying balustrades, he felt as if at any moment it might break free of its moorings, give a deafening blast on its foghorn and steam off into the west, a notion that, with the white mountains in the distance rising up into the deep blue sky, seemed to him as wonderful as it was ridiculous.

The hall was to seat four thousand people, a task that pushed architects, workmen and stage designers to the limit of their capabilities. The parquet flooring was ripped up and fresh concrete poured to prevent the wood from creaking beneath the weight of eight thousand patent leather shoes and high-heeled ankle boots. Stands, steps and podiums were stacked all the way to the roof. Screws, valves, bellows, pedals and pipes, all individually wrapped in linen and tissue paper, were wheeled over in handcarts and assembled into an organ as tall as a house. The podiums for orchestra and choir had to be stacked up and slotted into each other at different levels beforehand to accommodate the acoustics and sightlines; nothing should hinder the audience from listening to the orchestra, which had been enlarged to one hundred and eighty musicians, or the eight vocal soloists, five-hundred-strong choir and three hundred and fifty children from the Munich singing school.

'This work doesn't just border on delusions of grandeur,' screamed the front page of one of the big Munich newspapers. 'It aims to exceed them. The craving for the highest pinnacle knows no bounds. It will end in triumph or disaster: there is not, there cannot be, anything in between. But the story will be one for the ages: this is how it was, the Symphony of a Thousand!'

Gutmann had coined the phrase 'Symphony of a Thousand' months earlier, in order to boost sales and cement the concert's significance in the public consciousness, particularly that of newspaper editors. Mahler found it idiotic. He first heard of it in Toblach, and he slammed his fists on the table so hard that Alma's prettiest water jug fell to the floor and shattered with a dull crack. For a moment he stared down at the glistening mess at his feet, then he ran down to the post office and cabled Munich. 'What in God's name are you thinking, promoting this vulgar nonsense? Terminology of this kind should disqualify itself on principle. My music needs no fairground barker, and certainly not a crackpot idea like this.'

The impresario promised he would never pronounce the words 'Symphony of a Thousand' again, which he didn't find too hard as they had already had the desired effect: a huge rush for tickets and every last seat in the hall sold out. When the doors closed and Mahler ascended the podium, total silence fell. An hour later, when the last note had faded and he lowered the baton, wiped his hand across his dripping face and turned to the audience, the applause erupted and swelled to a tumult that shook the ceiling; damp with exhalation, it proceeded to rain droplets onto the heads and shoulders of three thousand people, all beside themselves with excitement.

Half a year had gone by since then; half a year like half a life. Yet the triumph of that moment was suddenly so present it seemed to Mahler he could still hear the cheers and applause. He thought of how he had stood on the podium, knees shaking, surrounded and besieged by laughing, crying people drunk with joy and admiration. He had searched for Alma's face in the crowd but couldn't spot it in the confusion of light and noise. He was alone with all that happiness.

The fever had him again. It was a strip of hot iron behind his forehead, radiating out all over his body. Only his fingers, clinging to the railing, were cold and stiff.

'There's nothing to be had up here,' he said out loud. 'Go away: I know who you are.'

For a moment he had thought the white bird was back, crouching a few metres behind him.

You can't rely on anything in this world, he thought. Least of all yourself.

The fever was high, but he didn't feel bad. It was easy to stand like this, leaning on the railing, and if the pain was consistent, he could bear it. He was encouraged to find that this was how he felt. It was possible to bear many things, and overall the voyage was going much as expected. No, that was wrong: he hadn't expected anything. They were going home, that was all. The only difference from previous voyages was that this would be his last. But he couldn't even say that for certain. What were once certainties were now just tales. Sentimental obituaries and anecdotes. Just before he had slipped the ring on Alma's finger in St Charles's Church, she had whispered 'for ever' in his ear. He had heard the words, and hadn't questioned them. He had believed in her absolutely, with the same awareness that, as a four-year-old Jewish boy, he had believed in the Christ Child, or Belial with eyes like coals. To believe was to know. Now, he knew nothing any more. The only thing he could always somehow rely on was his body, or rather its disintegration. The coughing-up of blood. The pain and the fever. The cold in his bones. The hard throbbing in his temples. That was reality. Outside, this unreal, bright, hot light everywhere; and underneath, below the surface, nothing but conjecture. Reality occurred deep within his body. He should have written it down. He should have composed his body's harmonies. The disharmonies even more so. Too late. The operas had spoiled music for him. He had made too little music in his life. That night, after the Munich concert, he had written something new. Good music, just a few notes, but at least it was a start. Once more. He'd had hopes of the winter in New York. There wasn't much left for him to do there, and the snow on the streets muffled sound. He liked to work when it was snowing. He liked it when the first snow fell, in total silence, on the autumn leaves in Central Park. Later, it turned grey from all the coal dust in the air. Perhaps the coal had hastened things. The doctors had their theories. Alma didn't like snow. She said it ruined her shoes. Although she did have twenty pairs. They went for evening walks in the park, where snowflakes caught in her hair and on her fur coat, and afterwards they went to bed. But it wasn't the same any more. She drank too much, and when he touched her, she was hard. Marble skin and glassy eyes. It wasn't the same, and they would go to sleep. Sometimes he dreamed that he was biting her. In his dream he tore great chunks of flesh from her body and gulped them down without chewing. When he woke, he was disgusted by himself and by his dreams, and went and walked the streets to find clarity in the cold. He yearned for clarity and simplicity. Our first thoughts are simple, and so are our last. It's just in between that everything gets lost. When he got back, she was lying there looking like a child. And he knew that, once again, he had been mistaken. Life was just one long series of mistakes. But here she lay, in the bluish light. And the other man was God knows where.

He thought of him now, the slim man with the too-big hat beneath the bridge. The dismay on their faces when they emerged from the room, and the train on which he had steamed out of the valley. Then he thought of the trains he himself had sat, worked and slept on. So many departures, never to arrive. Train journeys were nicer than voyages, though. The landscape kept changing; you just had to keep looking out of the window for long enough. The sea basically always stayed the same. It changed its face, but not its character. The sea is a whore. Who said that? Stop it; it's holding up forty thousand tonnes of steel. It's a whore. It's dirty and cold. I don't understand what the boy likes about it. He's a good boy, but it'll be the death of him. Perhaps, but you can't say a thing like that. Why not? That's what's at stake. Everything is at stake. There are no words for it. There are no words for life, none for death, and none for music. Stop it. Where was this leading? If he didn't watch out, things were threatening to get out of hand. Fever made you mad. He had to use all his concentration to get his bearings. The wind was coming at him from all sides. Clutching the cold metal with his cold fingers, he carefully eased himself up to take some weight off his legs. They felt shapeless and wobbly, but he just had to stretch his knees a few times and wiggle his toes and they soon felt better.

He looked around. He was alone.

Before heading back to New York, they had returned to Vienna. That city was no longer the same, either. He had stood beneath the windows of his old apartment and tried to picture how they had lived. He thought of the bathroom with the tiled walls and the nickel-plated taps above the bathtub. Alma used to bathe every day in winter. Half his Court Opera salary went on warm water. But there was her body beneath the surface of the water. With the children, sometimes. First one little girl, then the two of them. He couldn't remember ever seeing anything more beautiful than those soft, white bodies in the water. Like sea creatures, a female with her young. Strange that he should remember this only now. And the coke stove, crackling in the corner of the living room. This was where it had started. The first time he coughed up blood in Vienna. Once, he had sprinkled his sheet music with blood. A writer would have seized on this and had the tiny specks arrange themselves on the staves, as if by accident, into a usable theme, a wonderful melody, the start of a new movement or suchlike. But he wasn't a writer; he was a musician, and he was sick, and the blood just made a mess of his work. There are no coincidences, he thought. Everything is either work or destiny. The law of the fishes has no validity up here. Stand up straight. It's not yet time. They'll come soon enough, and then it'll be the same as always. Right now, though, it was good to be standing here.

'I should stay a bit longer,' he said out loud. But

already he could no longer hear his own voice. Nor did he notice his fingers loosening, or that, as he tried to lean a little further over the railing, he slumped and his knees hit the deck, seconds before the men's feet came clattering up the stairs; their voices, the warrant officer's harsh, clear instructions, the hands grabbing him, smelling of tar, and the arms that bore him off like a sleeping child, while away in the distance the water began to seethe, and just moments later a shoal of fish rose up, silver and shimmering and so gigantic it seemed to cast its shadow over the whole of the sea.

It was raining, and already dark. All day the boy had been loading oil drums and great pallets of cotton at the docks, and he was tired and frozen when he got to the harbour café. He sat at a table by the stove, ordered coffee with hot milk and slipped off his shoes, which were caked with dirt and whale oil. The café had no name; the dock workers met here because it was quieter than the harbour bars nearby, where sailors got drunk and there were arguments and fights every evening. The owner was a haggard German with a broken nose and sun-bleached, flaxen hair. He had poured concrete over the rotted wooden floor, replaced the smoke-blackened windows and exchanged the old paraffin lamps for modern electric lights, and since then the place was bright and friendly. Workers sat at the tables and bar, shoulders heavy, staring into their glasses. Two men were eating stew; it smelled of onions and burnt bacon. The boy stretched out his legs under the table and wiggled his toes. The fire in the stove was low; he took two logs from the pile and shoved them in. Here, in the warmth, he realised how tired he was. He was fifteen years old and as tired as an old man. But the coffee was strong and sweet, and it was nice to stare into the glowing flames and prod the ashes with the poker.

His gaze fell on the pile of old newspapers the café owner had collected for setting the fire. A copy of the *Brooklyn Citizen* lay on top. There was a photo of a man on the front page. To the boy, this face seemed like an apparition from another world, but he immediately recognised the little man who had sat, wrapped in blankets, on the sundeck of the *Amerika*. A long summer lay between the present day and his first, and last, voyage as a ridiculously smartly dressed ship's boy. When he had taken off the uniform in Cherbourg and returned it, brushed and starched, to the training officer, he had felt free for the first time in his life. He had signed up on a number of ships, including two turbine steamers and one of the last great three-masted clippers; he had scrubbed decks, shovelled coal, peeled potatoes and helped mend nets. When he arrived in New York at the end of the summer with a live cargo of northern German pigs, his hands, previously those of a child, were as cracked and hard as an old ropemaker's. For some time he had also been conscious of a peculiar internal swaying sensation that never left him, even at night, so he decided to earn his living for a while on the solid ground of the docks.

The man in the photo was undoubtedly the man from the sundeck, but he looked younger and stronger. He was glancing up slightly, with a rather penetrating stare. The boy picked up the paper and went over to the counter, where the German stood stirring his stew with a wooden spoon.

'Excuse me,' said the boy.

The German held his nose over the pot and sniffed. He took the pot off the heat, wiped his face with the corner of his apron, and turned to the boy. 'What is it?'

'Could you tell me what this says?' said the boy, putting the paper on the counter.

'That paper's five months old,' said the landlord.

'Never mind,' said the boy. 'For me it's fine.'

'Why don't you read it yourself?'

'I don't know any English.'

'Then you should learn. A man is nothing without language.'

'Yes,' said the boy. 'Now please will you read it?'

The landlord smoothed out the paper with his

large hands, leant forward and narrowed his eyes. After a while he sat up again and looked the boy in the face. 'The man's dead.'

'Thought so,' said the boy, and nodded.

'His heart gave out.'

'Yes,' said the boy quietly.

'Did you know him?' asked the landlord.

'No,' said the boy. 'Only a little.'

The landlord looked at the boy suspiciously, then lowered his eyes again to the paper.

'The funeral was on the twenty-second of May. There was a big crowd. Lots of famous people. His wife didn't attend. It rained, and the wind blew blossom from the trees.'

'That must have looked nice.'

'It says here that he made music. He was a proper musician, this man of yours.'

'He was a director.'

'It doesn't say that here.'

'He was, though,' said the boy firmly.

'Maybe,' said the landlord. 'And now he's dead. He's with the Lord, or elsewhere. Nothing to be done about it.'

'No,' said the boy. 'Nothing to be done.'

The landlord folded the paper and pushed it across the counter. 'You can have it,' he said. 'Present from me.'

The boy shook his head. He didn't touch the paper.

'It's a crying shame,' said the landlord, 'that it always has to be like this in this godforsaken world.'

Outside, on the street, it was still raining. A cold, grey, relentless autumn rain. The boy walked past the great warehouses to the lodgings he shared with forty other workers. Men with upturned collars passed him in the dark, on their way to a bar or their sleeping quarters. He stopped under a canopy and stood there for a while, listening to the patter of the rain. He thought of the man on the sundeck. He had almost forgotten him, and now he was dead. He would have liked to have heard his music. It was sure to be nothing like the music he knew, the screeching violins in the harbour bars or the sounds squeezed from the accordion of the engineer with whom he had sailed twice across the Baltic. The dead man's music was something different. He imagined it to be something great and unpredictable. What a pity, he thought, that now it's lost for ever.

The street was completely empty now, and the boy continued on his way. The rain poured down, and he began to run; he heard his feet slapping on the wet pavement and looked forward to the warmth of the barracks. He would lie down on his bed, press his face into the gap between mattress and wall and abandon himself to his dreams. By morning, if not before, it would have stopped raining; the day was sure to be cool and bright. And that was good, because it was time to go.

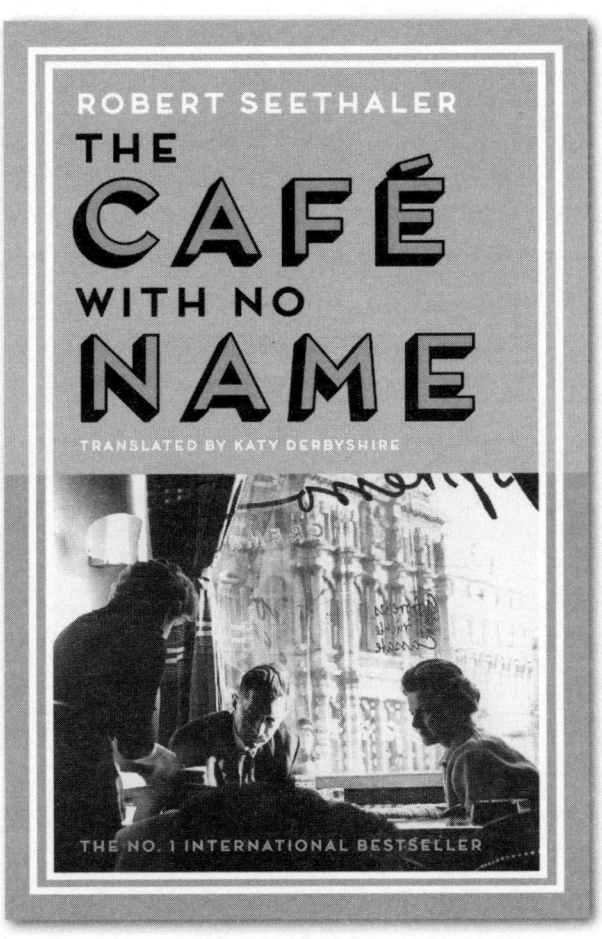

'[Seethaler's] latest fable-like miniature invites quiet wonder into the ordinary' *Financial Times*

CANON‖GATE

TURN THE PAGE FOR AN EXTRACT
FROM THE NUMBER ONE INTERNATIONAL BESTSELLER
THE CAFÉ WITH NO NAME

THE CAFÉ WITH NO NAME

ROBERT SEETHALER

TRANSLATED BY KATY DERBYSHIRE

CANONGATE

1.

At four-thirty on a Monday morning, Robert Simon left his lodgings in war widow Martha Pohl's flat. It was the late summer of 1966 and Simon was thirty-one years old. He had breakfasted alone – two boiled eggs, bread and butter, and black coffee. The widow had still been asleep; he'd heard quiet snores from her room. He liked the sound, found it strangely touching, and sometimes he cast a glance through the crack of the door to where he pictured the old woman's nostrils flaring in the darkness.

Down on the street, the wind hit him. When it came from the south the breeze carried with it the market's stench, the smell of rubbish and rotting fruit, but today it came from the west and the air was fresh and cool. Simon passed the grey housing block for retired tram workers, Schneeweis & Sons' metal workshop and a row of shops, all of them still closed. He cut down Malzgasse to Leopoldsgasse and, crossing Schiffamtsgasse, reached the short end of Haidgasse. On the corner, he stopped to take a look inside the former market café. He leaned his forehead against the glass and screwed up his eyes to see clearly. Chairs and tables were stacked in front of the big black counter. The wallpaper was faded and bulging in places; it looked as if the walls had faces. The plaster needs air, Simon thought. The windows would have to stay open for a few days before he started painting. The mustiness and damp. The old shadows and the dust. He pushed himself back from the glass, turned around and crossed the road to the market, where Johannes Berg was raising the shutters of his butcher's shop with a great clatter.

'Morning,' said the butcher. 'You can hack a couple of blocks of ice for me, if you like.'

'I've got enough to do with the veg,' Simon said. 'Nineteen crates of swedes.'

The butcher shrugged and set about extending his awning, twisting a long rod in the mechanism. He was sweating, the back of his neck shining in the early-morning sun.

'I'll grease those hinges for you later, if you want,' Simon offered.

'I can do that myself.'

'You used rancid lard on them last winter. You could smell them all the way to the Prater come spring.'

'It wasn't lard, it was suet.'

'Just let me know if you want any help,' said Simon. 'I can do it later. Won't take long.'

'Right you are,' said the butcher. He unhooked the rod, placed it next to the front entrance and wiped his hands on his bloodstained apron. His face looked soft in the filtered light beneath the red-and-white-striped fabric.

'We've got a nice day ahead,' he said. 'Plenty of sun but not too hot.'

'You're right there,' said Simon. 'See you later.'

Robert Simon was a gaunt man with sinewy arms and long, thin legs. His face was tanned from working in the open air; his ash-blond hair flopped over his brow. His hands were large and strewn with scars, the kind you get from working with rough wooden crates. His eyes were blue. They were the only handsome thing about him.

He walked more slowly than usual as various stallholders raised a hand or called out a friendly word or two. It was his seventh year on the market and today was his last day, and as they watched him stroll past they didn't know whether to be pleased or sad for him.

At the loading dock, he heaved crates of swedes and onions onto his shoulders and carried them over to Navracek's fruit and veg stall. He snipped green from the onions and sprouts from the potatoes, restacked winter firewood so it wouldn't go mouldy, and piled up empty pallets. At the fishmonger's, he cleaned scales, slime and blood off the ice tubs. He stuffed dirtied ice and fish heads with their staring eyes and gaping mouths in a sack and lugged it to the rubbish. Later, he went to the stall selling toys, wooden cars and brightly painted tin carousels, where he cleaned the rust off the latticed floor with a scraper. He had always enjoyed his work: the variety, the physical effort, the tips that jangled in his pockets at the end of the day. He liked the cold clear winter air, the summer's heat that softened the asphalt enough for bottle tops to sink into it; he liked the stallholders' hoarse voices as they shouted over each other, and the idea that he was a small part of a living, breathing, noisy organism.

Before the market closed, he went back to the butcher's. He'd picked up a jar of grease at the ironmonger's to lubricate the awning's joints. He dipped a finger in the grease and spread it on the hinges and the threads of the adjusting screw. He took his time over the job, rubbing and dabbing at the screw until his fingertips hurt.

'You keep on like that and you'll rub right through the metal,' the butcher said. He took a wallet out of the knife drawer and pulled out a note, his fingers clumsy.

'Forget it,' said Simon.

The butcher shrugged and put his money away again. 'You can come back any time,' he said. 'There's always work for a man like you.'

'Thanks.'

'I wish you luck. But I'll be seeing you anyway.'

'Oh, yes,' said Simon. 'You'll be seeing me.'

That evening, he didn't walk home his usual way. He took the narrow Leopoldstadt streets via Praterstrasse and Vorgartenstrasse up to the Danube, where freight ships and barges dipped out of the shadow of Reich Bridge, gliding upstream in the glistening evening sunlight. As he reached the old machine shop, he broke into a run. He ran along the towpath, past enormous hunks of concrete, past dump sites, scrap heaps and rusty iron fences. Driftwood and swollen cardboard boxes slopped against the riverbank. Gulls screeched high above him, and over the grassy strip on the north bank of the Danube, suburban children's kites painted tiny bright dabs on the sky. He ran, panting, his mouth open and his arms flailing. Sweat ran down his face and his heart thudded hard in his throat. He squinted towards the sun and saw the café with its dusty seating area before him, the tables and chairs in the failing light, the faces on the wallpapered brickwork, and as he ran on, stumbling, a stabbing in his lungs – under Augarten Bridge, up a washed-out embankment, over hot, crunching gravel and past black rushes and scrub with scraps of paper fluttering on its thorns – he felt he could run that way for ever.